The School for Gifted Potentials

Revelations

By Allis Wade

To Lillian and Allison
for your advice and encouragement
and
For my mom
Thank you for your love and support

Acknowledgements

I would like to acknowledge Kazimierz Dabrowski and his Theory of Positive Disintegration, along with other theorists that have contributed to gifted education, which provided much of the impetus for this book.

Praise for **Orientation**: The School for Gifted Potentials, Volume 1

"In her book, Orientation: The School for Gifted Potentials, Allis Wade has skillfully brought together the factual research of a past psychologist with a prospective world of the future, to create a unique book available in today's gifted world: a novel. It is simply refreshing to take a break from textbooks and journals to find oneself riding an emotional roller coaster along with the characters in the book."-**Melinda Gindy, Board Director: Australian Association for the Education of the Gifted and Talented**

"The purpose of this book is to give gifted children a chance to see and better understand themselves in modern literature. They may relate to some of the overexcitabilities described, and even utilize some of the coping mechanisms. Also, gifted children may identify with the attempt to hide their abilities out of a desire to fit in. They may become more willing to accept who they are and what they're capable of becoming."-**Sarah Wilson, Homeschool Review**

Praise for **Revelations**: The School for Gifted Potentials, Volume 2

"The students are all away from home, managing new levels of self-awareness and abilities. Teachers are mentors, but can be quite mysterious. Friends create conflict, but also offer insight into each others' personalities. In fact, the group of friends is one of the most interesting aspects of the stories. Although each is identified as "gifted," their personalities, strengths, and passions are all across the map, giving an accurate representation of the actual gifted population."-**Ian Byrd, Byrdseed Gifted**

"Revelations lives up to its title. There are many answers revealed from the first book, but just as many new questions are raised. The tangled web woven by his mother begins to unravel as the reader learns the truth behind Everett's admission to the SFGP. But ... all is not as it appears at the School for Gifted Potentials!"-**Lisa Conrad, Gifted Parenting Support**

Table of Contents

Reflection

Everett walked back to his room at a leisurely pace, thinking back on his first week of academic classes at The School for Gifted Potentials.

Two weeks before, Everett had lived a secure but secluded life with his mother. She had trained him from a young age to hide his gifted traits, knowing that a Government Observer could find him and require him to test at The School for Gifted Potentials. Children enrolled in the school were required to live there, and he and his mother had vowed to stay together, no matter how miserable he was at his school for AVERAGE learners.

To his great surprise and despair, his mother had deserted him at the school on his testing day, leaving him with questions about her reasons for raising him to hide his gifted traits and anger over her abandonment. Nothing could have prepared him to find out that his mother had been a student at the school herself, or that she had lied to him about her identity. He even found out that she had earned the G tattoo, a coveted symbol given to graduates of the school, but had never taken it.

Despite uncovering these disturbing secrets about his mother's past, Everett had thrived during his one week ORIENTATION at the school. He had learned about his OVEREXCITABILITIES and was already using some of the strategies that he had learned to manage them.

The best part of his ORIENTATION had been finding other children that he liked, and respected, and he was now part of a small, devoted group of friends.

Shaking his head at these thoughts, Everett scanned his badge to open the door to his room and stepped inside. It had become second nature to him to order his dinner before stepping into a hot shower the moment that he walked in the door, and he was walking to the screen to place his order when he noticed a pile of rolled up papers on his table.

Surprised, he walked over to his table and found a note.

Dear Everett,

I hope that you had a wonderful first week of classes. You asked me about personalizing your room, and I thought that these posters from my office would give you a good start. Feel free to use any of them to hang on your wall.

Take care,

Sindra

The unexpected gifts touched Everett. Sindra had been his mentor during his ORIENTATION, but she was also the Observer that had initially discovered him and was the reason that he had been forced to test at the school. Despite his initial resentment and distrust for Sindra, they had grown to understand each other during his ORIENTATION, and it felt good to know that she was still thinking about him.

Eagerly fishing through the pile, Everett found the poster that he really wanted, the poster showing Landon Perry and the INTELLEX crew landing on Mars. He was deeply interested in the astronaut, especially since he had learned that the astronaut had been his mother's friend during her MASTERY studies at The School for Gifted Potentials.

He placed the large poster on the wall directly across from his bed and stood back to study it for a few moments. A strange feeling washed over him as he studied Landon's handsome face and dark eyes, and he turned to look through the rest of the posters feeling unsettled.

After selecting the ICOTTS poster because he liked the picture and a small photograph of an elderly woman posing next to a solar powered airplane, he took the rest of the posters and stuffed them behind his desk. He did not really want them, but figured that they might be useful to have around at some point.

With the posters taken care of, he logged in his meal preference for the night and hopped into the shower. As the hot water poured over him, he visualized the water flooding into his body, melting away the lingering tension from the day. It was a modified version of the visualization exercise that he learned in his ORIENTATION. He had found a way to combine the relaxation technique with his daily shower, which shaved off a little time that he could use for his evening assignments.

After changing into his luxurious sleeping clothes and scarfing down a warm spinach salad, he grabbed his SKEtch pad and pulled up a video message from Ms. Everlay, his life science instructor, expecting an evening assignment.

"Congratulations Everett! You have completed your first week of academic classes. You will have a day of rest tomorrow to relax, study, and socialize. On the following day, you will take your first INTENSIVE. For the first two months of your academic classes, your instructors will assign you to an INTENSIVE class each week, but after we have exposed you to a variety of options, you will select INTENSIVES based on your interests. I have selected a dramatic expression class for your first INTENSIVE because Mr. Dodd shared your interest in this area with us. After your class, please create a brain bridge or write a reflection about what you learned. Be sure to include a description of what you *felt*. I am intrigued by the experiment that you designed this week, and I look forward to seeing you next week."

Ms. Everlay signed off with a wave and a smile.

Everett grinned and stretched out on his bed. Kimin had mentioned something about the INTENSIVE classes. Some students already had an identified STRENGTH in PSYCHOMOTOR ABILITY or VISUAL and PERFORMING ARTS when they enrolled at the SFGP. Everett's friend Sonniy was already an accomplished cello player because a private tutor had been coaching her for many years. The INTENSIVE classes helped all of the Gifted Potentials discover new STRENGTHS and interests.

Placing his hands behind his head, Everett thought about his brief experience with the PERFORMING ARTS in Mr. Dodd's class, where he had watched a video of a young girl utterly transform herself into an elderly man. Her performance had stirred something deep inside of him, and he had vowed that he would find a way to become a part of that magic. The fact that Mr. Dodd had played a part in getting him the opportunity to experience it right away made him feel a swell of emotion.

He still felt a deep connection to the instructor that had helped him discover his OVEREXCITABILITIES and gifted CHARACTERISTICS. Everett's EMOTIONAL OE caused him to develop strong bonds with other people, and he missed his instructor deeply.

Rolling his head around to relieve the tension that had built as he thought about Mr. Dodd, Everett's eyes landed on the poster of the INTELLEX crew. As he twisted to get a better look at the poster, he thought back to Landon Perry's connection with his mother. Everett had been raised to believe that his mother's name was Mae Davidson and that she was a chef and a single mother. She had raised him to think that The School for Gifted Potentials was a place that she had to protect him from, and she had coached him to appear AVERAGE to his teachers and classmates so that he would not be forced to go there.

After years of pretending to struggle academically in classes that were actually remedial for him, an Observer in disguise had tricked Everett into showing his mathematical STRENGTH, which had resulted in a mandatory testing session at the school. Everett had arrived prepared to fail the tests and go home with his mother, only to discover that she had signed the papers that allowed the school to keep him.

Just as he had come to terms with his mother's choice to leave him at the school, Everett had discovered that his mother had actually gone to the SFGP, that she had lied about her identity, and that she had played a major role in the creation of the Life and Natural Sciences Wing, along with Landon Perry.

Once he had found out that his mother's real name was Camilla Grey and that she was the sister of the Chancellor, his feelings about being abandoned had changed. Although he now understood why his mother had thought that she should give him the opportunity to attend the school and had forgiven her for her choice, he had not come to terms with the lies that she had told him about herself.

Feeling a bitter pain radiating through him at these thoughts, Everett took several deep breaths to calm himself down. Knowing that it usually took some time to settle down after thoughts of his mother upset him, he decided to call Greta, his best friend at the SFGP.

She shared his interests in science and nature, and they both had the INTELLECTUAL OVEREXCITABILITY, so they spent a lot of time discussing their ideas and questions with each other, or at least what time they could spare.

Greta had finished her ORIENTATION before Everett, and he had worried that the connection they had made would be lost once they started their academic classes, but he had been pleased to discover that she was in his life science class. Although they were both overwhelmed by the workload that came with their classes, they had still found time during their first week to eat lunch together and to video conference at night.

Everett jumped off his bed to call Greta, and she answered right away.

"Hey Greta! I just got a message about my INTENSIVE for this week. I am enrolled in dramatic expression. Mr. Dodd must have noticed how excited I was about acting when he presented the VISUAL and PERFORMING ARTS to us."

Greta smiled softly and leaned toward the camera.

"That's a great choice for you Everett. I am enrolled in an INTENSIVE to learn how to play wind instruments. I can't wait. I have always pictured myself sitting in the middle of a forest, playing a flute by a babbling brook."

She flushed as she shared this thought with him. She also had the IMAGINATIONAL OVEREXCITABILITY and had a vivid imagination. Everett nodded and smiled reassuringly at her, knowing that it was hard for her to share personal information with others.

"Are you going to study all day tomorrow?" he asked hesitantly.

The friends that he had made during his ORIENTATION had not gotten together as a whole group since their academic classes had started, and he realized that Kimin and Sonniy had never even met CiCi. Everett wanted to set up a time the next day to get together with all of his friends, but he wanted to check with Greta first. If she felt too anxious about completing her assignments, he did not want to pressure her into taking time away from her work.

To his surprise, she shook her head with a smile.

"I need to work on my assignments, and I already have ideas about what I want to accomplish, but I also miss Kimin, Sonniy, Jeremiah, Kabe, and CiCi. I was sort of hoping that we could get together with them," she replied shyly.

"Sounds great!" he replied, glad that she had been the one to make the suggestion. "Give me a minute and I will set it up!"

She nodded and waved goodbye as their connection ended.

He immediately called Kimin to set up a time. She had been thinking the same thing and had already asked Sonniy, Jeremiah, and Kabe. He told her about CiCi, and she looked jealous for a moment before she airily told him that he could invite anyone he wanted. They arranged to meet on the patio after breakfast and then waved goodbye.

Everett felt a little uncomfortable as he called CiCi and Greta to tell them the plan. He realized that Kimin wanted a reunion of the friends that she had made during *her* ORIENTATION and might be upset that her friends had gone on to befriend someone that she did not know. After a few moments, he recalled Sindra's advice for avoiding conflict with his friends. If he wanted to be sure that his actions did not offend them, he should be open with them and ask them about their expectations.

With that in mind, he called Kimin again. Her smile was slightly confused when she saw him on her screen since they had just talked.

"Kimin, I felt like you were a little upset that I want to invite CiCi tomorrow. I was hoping that you would try to get to know her, but I don't want you to feel like you have to. I could always meet up with her at a different time if it bothers you to invite her," he said sincerely, although he was hoping that she would agree to include the little girl.

Kimin frowned as she thought about his words. She liked to be in control, but she realized that she and Sonniy were the only people in the group that did not know CiCi, and there was no good reason to exclude the little girl.

Smiling sheepishly, she replied, "I appreciate that you checked with me Everett. I guess I was a little jealous. You can bring your friend, and I will include her. See you tomorrow!"

She signed off with a wink.

Everett went to his desk and pulled out his SKEtch pad, relieved that he had taken the time to make sure that Kimin was not upset and excited about having a reunion with all of his friends. He had spent time with his friends throughout the week, although never all together. Their schedule allowed them one hour, twice a day, for recreation, eating, and studying, and his friends had all given themselves different amounts of time for each activity.

After settling cross-legged onto his bed, he activated his SKEtch pad and pulled up his file of data from the planetarium. He quickly became absorbed in putting the data into the brain bridge that he had started earlier in the week. Finding patterns and categorizing information was both stimulating and calming for Everett.

Once he had entered the planetarium data for each day and night that week, he pulled up the file that contained weather information and carefully added it to his bridge. Once that was complete, he started browsing through the local, national, and world news to see if anything looked important enough to add.

Everett had been charting this kind of information for over a year and was not sure what he was looking for. Researching the cultures of ancient peoples had led him to discover that they had predicted calamities, important births, and other notable events from the patterns that they saw in the stars, and he had become fascinated by the idea that the stars could forecast major events. So far, his data had not shown him much, but he knew that it might take him many years to see a pattern. His INTELLECTUAL OVEREXCITABILITY created this drive to learn and understand and gave him the energy to pursue an interest for many years.

After two hours of charting data, he finally decided to go to sleep. He dimmed his lights and crawled into bed feeling proud that he had completed his first week of classes at The School for Gifted Potentials.

Reunion

The next morning, Everett gulped down a healthy breakfast of egg whites and vegetables before heading out of his room. On days when students did not have classes, a soft cotton shirt in royal blue replaced the formal white shirt and sweater vest uniform. The new shirt put an unexpected bounce in his step, and he found himself grinning with anticipation at the reunion with his friends. His pace quickened as he neared the patio, both eager and nervous to have his whole group together again.

He was disappointed to find that only Kabe was there when he arrived. The other boy gave him a nod of welcome before he turned back to look over the railing at the panoramic view of the land that surrounded the school. Everett joined him and leaned his forearms on the railing as he drew the cool morning air into his lungs.

The awkward silence between the boys did not last long because Kimin and Sonniy soon burst through the doors, talking and laughing loudly. They were followed closely by Jeremiah, who looked sleepy and rumpled, and Greta, whose long, loose royal blue cotton dress looked pressed and pristine. As the group greeted one another and chatted happily, Everett looked around for CiCi, hoping that his young friend would make it to the gathering.

She arrived just as the group was settling into chairs at a long table at the end of the patio. She bounced over to Kabe's side and greeted him with a light hug, then stood awkwardly at his side, twisting her hands as she looked at Kimin and Sonniy.

After only a moment of hesitation, Kimin went over to the younger girl and shook her hand.

"Hi! I'm Kimin and that's Sonniy," she said, pointing to her friend, who gave the little girl a small wave. "We were in your friends' ORIENTATION classes before you arrived, and they have already told us a lot about you."

CiCi smiled her warm, dimpled smile and slipped her hand into Kimin's. Kimin beamed at the sweet gesture and pulled the little girl into a chair between her and Sonniy. Everett could see with relief that the young girl's gesture had won Kimin over, and both Kimin and Sonniy were now touching CiCi's long golden hair as they chatted with her about her classes.

Relieved that his friends were now chatting harmoniously, Everett leaned back and let the conversation flow around him. He and his friends all had very different schedules, but it sounded as though everyone was enthusiastic about what they were learning. When the topic of INTENSIVES came up, Everett sat forward, interested in hearing which class everyone else had been assigned to.

"I'm not really happy about my INTENSIVE," Sonniy whined with her arms crossed.

"Why not?" CiCi asked.

Her face screwed into an expression of concern, and she placed a gentle hand on Sonniy's arm.

"Well, I already have a STRENGTH in MUSIC. I am an expert cello player. My instructor said that she wants me to do an INTENSIVE in sculpture. I think that I should get to do an INTENSIVE on a different string instrument," she answered with a pout.

"Well, the INTENSIVES that our instructors pick for us the first two months are supposed to expose us to things that we might be interested in, or that we haven't tried before, so that we can see the variety of options that we have at this school. Once you finish the two months, you can pick another string instrument if you want to, but you could also find out that there is something that you love even more," Kimin replied somewhat reprovingly.

"Let's go around the table and tell which INTENSIVE we were assigned to," CiCi suggested excitedly.

The group nodded and eagerly shared their assignments. Kabe would be in a martial arts class, Jeremiah was assigned to a problem solving class, Greta would be in a wind instruments class, Kimin had an animal enrichment class, and CiCi was also assigned to the sculpture class.

The conversation drifted again as discussions between pairs and small groups ebbed and flowed. Everett was listening to Jeremiah describe his struggles with understanding a math formula that he had been taught when his attention was pulled away by something that Sonniy was saying.

She was complaining to Greta that Dre also played the cello and that the *original* had been rude to her behind their instructor's back. Dre was the head of a group of students called the *originals* that had lived at The School for Gifted Potentials since they were infants. They believed that growing up at the SFGP had given them an edge over students that started as children, who they called *transplants*.

Dre was vocal about the fact that she believed that a *transplant* could never be as good as an *original*. According to Sonniy, she and Dre had a private instructor because they were too advanced for the other classes. It wounded Dre's pride to have a younger student, and a *transplant*, match her abilities.

Everyone listened to her complaint intently because they were all concerned about how they had been treated by the *originals* during their ORIENTATION. Greta shyly filled Sonniy and Kimin in on the plan that the group had made to deal with the *originals*. They had realized that hiding from them as individuals would just ensure that the *originals* kept bullying them, so they had decided to stand up to the bullies as a group. Jeremiah jumped in excitedly to tell how his friends had stood up for him in the dining hall when two *originals* had cornered him and smiled as he recalled that the *originals* had avoided them later in the hallway.

Kimin frowned with concern as she said, "I don't know if that was the best idea. Maybe they'll just keep tormenting us now, even though our ORIENTATIONS are over. I think that you should have just left them alone."

"Is that why Dre is so mean to me? Because you made the *originals* mad at us?" Sonniy asked plaintively.

Greta and Jeremiah exchanged a concerned look, but Kabe jumped in to express his opinion with confidence.

"Look Sonniy, you and Kimin weren't there when we stood up to them, and Dre wasn't even one of the *originals* that we stood up to, so I doubt that it's connected. I think that she is bullying you just because you are a *transplant*, and she thinks that she should always be better than a *transplant*, at anything. I think that it's time that someone shows the *originals* that their behavior is wrong, and I guess we are the *transplants* to do it."

The slow, confident smile on Kabe's face as he leaned back in his chair with his arms crossed quieted any further concerns.

Greta stood up and smoothed her skirt. There was a pained look on her face, but she seemed unable to speak. Realizing that she was probably starting to get worried about finishing her assignments, Everett jumped up and addressed the group for her.

"Well, it has been great to get to see you all as a whole group, but I think that I should go to my room for a while to work on some projects. Would anybody like to get together later to eat and then go to the rec center?" he asked, looking at Greta out of the corner of his eye.

The flush on Greta's face showed that he had read her concern correctly, and Sonniy and Kabe looked relieved by his suggestion as well.

"Yeah, I'd like to meet back here for the midday meal. I need to get some work done, but I know that I'll need a good break around that time," Kabe replied and hopped out of his chair.

The others looked around the table and nodded slowly. Kimin looked the most upset about the abrupt end to their socializing. After agreeing on a time to meet, the group slowly disbanded.

Jeremiah fell into step with Kabe as he left. CiCi joined hands with Sonniy and Kimin, and the trio chatted merrily as they walked down the hall.

Greta and Everett hung back for a moment and watched their friends leave. They shared a smile as they turned to rest their elbows on the railing and spent a few quiet moments soaking in the sun and fresh air. Greta stirred first, although reluctantly, and they headed back to their dormitories in amicable silence.

Greta's room came first, and Everett waved at her as she passed through her doorway and then turned down his hallway to head into his room. He was greeted with a view of Landon Perry as he entered his room, which startled him somewhat since he had entered the room with his mind on his science assignment.

As excited as he had been about receiving the poster, a strange new feeling had begun to twist his stomach each time that he looked at it. After a moment of hesitation, he pulled the poster down and switched it to the wall behind his bed. That way, he would not feel like the astronaut was staring at him from every angle in the room.

Satisfied with the change, Everett ordered a tall glass of ice water to sip on and pulled out his SKEtch pad. A thrill coursed through him as he pulled up the data from a science experiment that he had begun earlier in the week.

Combining his passion for studying plant and animal adaptations with his interest in Mars had been easy. After researching the conditions that had been reported by the crews on Mars, Everett had developed an experiment with his life science instructor to see which plants currently living in extreme habitats on Earth could survive in conditions similar to those on Mars.

He had set up a controlled experiment using an apparatus that could send him temperature, moisture, and growth data in real time for each plant that he was testing. He had selected a variety of seeds and had created a soil mixture that mimicked the content of the soil samples that had been sent back from Mars. The amount of light in the lab room was designed to simulate the sunlight on Mars.

In all, he had set up twenty-five test plants, and graphing and analyzing the data took him quite a while. Once he completed his graphing, he wrote down a few questions that he wanted to ask his instructor, along with some ideas that had formed as he examined the data.

I wonder why none of my seeds have sprouted yet, he thought. *Maybe I need to adjust the soil.*

He took a huge swallow of the now lukewarm water that had sat forgotten on the table and stood up to stretch. After checking the time, he was startled to realize that he only had a few minutes before he had to leave to meet his friends. His rumbling stomach urged him forward as he quickly checked his timeline and noted what other assignments he would need to work on once he got back to his room. He gulped down the rest of his water and practically ran to the patio.

Once again, he and Kabe were the first to arrive, but the others followed quickly. After a flurry of activity as everyone brought their food and beverages to the table, they all settled into a relatively quiet meal. Conversation was optional because they were all so comfortable with one another. Small conversations started as their eating slowed.

Everett told CiCi and Greta about his star data. CiCi was curious about how he got the data but did not understand his explanation because the planetarium had not been on one of her tours.

Greta was about to ask him a question about his research when Kimin leaned over her and said, "So, did you hear about the *celebrity* speaker that is coming in two weeks?"

As she had expected, her question got everyone's complete attention. After allowing them to ask for more information several times, she finally held up her hands to stop them.

"The special guest is... Landon Perry!" she squealed and clapped her hands, elated that she had been able to surprise her friends with the news.

Although the others in the group did not have an intense interest in Perry like Everett, they all knew about him and the INTELLEX crew. A flurry of excited chatter about the most popular graduate of the SFGP ensued, but Everett found that for some reason, he did not want to talk about the astronaut with his friends. His stomach churned at the thought of being in the same building with Landon Perry, although he did not want to consider the reason for his strange reaction. A week ago, he would have jumped out of his seat with excitement over the news, but instead, he shoved his hands deep into his pockets and moved away from his friends to look over the railing.

Greta noted the change in Everett's behavior, but she knew her friend well enough not to probe him about his feelings at the moment. Instead, she went to his side and gently pulled him away from his thoughts by telling him that the group was cleaning up to go to the rec center. He nodded and absently trailed behind the group as they headed to their favorite place. The group scattered to different activities as they entered.

Part of Everett wanted to tackle the climbing structure that he had discovered during his ORIENTATION, but he noticed that Greta had lingered in the center of the room, and he knew that she was hoping that he would join her in the Nature Center. He realized that spending time in nature with his best friend was a better choice than brooding alone at the top of the climbing structure, so he jogged up to her and asked her to join him in the Nature Center with a smile.

Nodding happily, she followed him with a casual jog as they hurried over to the Nature Center. MASTERY students had fully replaced the biome, and the South American rainforest had given way to a frozen tundra. Protective garments were located just inside of the netted enclosure, and Greta and Everett bundled up quickly because the deep chill had already begun to make them shiver. After their protective gear had begun to ward off the cold air, they stepped carefully into a vast, treeless space covered in snow.

Everett had spent very little time in the rec center during his first week of classes, but it was soon apparent that Greta had already spent a lot of time in the new environment. Stepping carefully, she wound past a few scrubby bushes before she pulled Everett down to examine a burrow. They spent nearly an hour in silent exploration. The vibrant sounds of running water and chattering animals that had made conversation possible in the rainforest had been replaced by the vast silence of the windy plains. After making eye contact and nodding toward the exit, they hurried out of their warm clothing and left the enclosure.

A quick search confirmed that their friends had already left, and Greta and Everett exchanged a sheepish smile when they realized how much time they had spent in the Nature Center. A flush crossed Greta's cheeks as she began to worry about finishing her assignments, so Everett ushered her back to her room so that she could work.

He realized that Greta worried about her schoolwork more than he did. Based on what Greta had shared about her assignments, she enjoyed what she was studying, so he was not sure what troubled her about her workload. He was usually the one that initiated the video calls each night. Although she seemed happy to be talking to him, he always sensed an impatience or nervousness emanating from her. She paid attention to what he was saying, but her eyes would often drift away as if she was looking at the work that she needed to complete rather than giving him her full focus. Meals were the same. Once her food was gone, she rarely liked to linger, whereas he would much rather stay and talk with her than go back to his room to study.

I wonder if her instructors give her more work to do than mine do or if we just worry about different things, he thought as he turned down the hallway to his room.

Troubled Dreams

Greta was still on his mind as he entered his room, and he frowned with concern as he grabbed his SKEtch pad and turned it on. After checking his plant data, he logged into a message from his technical writing instructor and sighed. Technical writing was his identified area of weakness. He had never really enjoyed writing and especially did not like to embellish his writing. Sometimes he felt like he just understood information. It was difficult for him to pull out the individual pieces of information that had melded together in some difficult to understand process in his mind and explain his thinking to other people.

In just one short week, however, his instructor had begun to show him not just *how* to write clearly and add detail, but also *why* it was important. He scanned through the critique that his instructor had written about his first technical writing piece and paced as he read her comments.

His assignment was to describe how he had set up his science experiment. It had taken him all week to write down the materials that he had used and the steps that he had taken to set up each of the twenty-five plants. His instructor had explained that it was important to write down how the experiment was set up, his reasons for setting it up that way, and his hypotheses about what might happen. Other scientists should not only know what steps to follow in order to repeat his experiments, but they should also know the reasoning behind each step. While that made good sense to Everett, it had been difficult for him to explain his thinking in writing.

The feedback from his teacher was that he needed to edit and revise his work. He had left out some steps, had repeated others, and had included very few reasons in his explanation. After looking through his work a few times, he found himself out of ideas and decided to shake off some of his nervous energy.

For a reason that he did not understand, he found himself at Kabe's door and knocked uncertainly. After a few moments, a surprised Kabe opened the door. He smiled when he saw Everett and gestured for him to enter the room. The first thing that Everett noticed was that the opposite wall had an intricate structure of metal rods attached to it. Kabe smiled and explained that it was the structure that he had designed with Mr. Elan when they had talked about the PSYCHOMOTOR OE. Kabe showed Everett how he could do sit-ups, pull-ups, or push-ups on the structure depending on where he gripped the rods. He could also climb up it or across it. A grin cracked Everett's face as he watched his friend's demonstration. He had to appreciate the other boy's ingenuity in managing his OE.

After playing on the equipment for a while, Everett invited Kabe to go with him to the rec center. Kabe looked surprised and mentioned that they had already been there that day.

Everett shrugged.

"I know. I just have some nervous energy to burn off, and I don't really feel like working on my assignment," he explained with a nervous grin.

Kabe nodded understandingly but said, "Sorry, I really can't. I want to finish my report. Why don't you ask Greta to go with you?"

Everett shook his head. "No, I don't think that Greta would be comfortable giving up any work time either. She really seems to worry about her assignments."

"She seems to worry about lots of things," Kabe agreed.

Pursing his lips at Kabe's observation, Everett waved goodbye as he left Kabe's room and headed back to his hallway. He realized that none of his friends would be taking a break from their work that evening, which told him that he probably should get back to his.

A few ideas came to him as he walked back to his room. When his door opened, he bolted inside and quickly added his ideas to his writing. He had realized as he walked that his technical writing assignment would not be so hard if he just pretended that he was explaining his experiment to Greta. She would not just want to know how he had set it up, she would also be curious about why he had set it up that way.

Feeling inspired, Everett wrote for over an hour. A dry mouth was the only thing that made him stop, and he realized that he needed to order his evening meal.

Energized by the work that he had done on his writing assignment, he logged in an order for a big meal and a warm cup of milk before he jumped into a quick shower. The comforting meal was waiting for him when he stepped back into the room, and he ate it quickly, feeling famished even though he had already eaten two large meals that day. He deposited his tray and dishes into the trash receptacle and then sat down to glance through his plant data to see if there had been any plant growth.

A new wave of interest in his assignments coursed through him, and he eagerly delved back into his star data, plant data, and his technical writing assignment. An unexpected yawn broke his momentum, and he was surprised to find that he had spent nearly three hours working, but the time had passed swiftly because he was so engaged in his projects. Regretfully, he turned off his SKEtch pad and climbed into bed.

It did not take Everett long to fall asleep, but his dreams caused him to toss and turn. In one dream, Landon Perry was at The School for Gifted Potentials, but he was very old. The entire student body was seated in a cavernous auditorium, and Everett was seated in the middle of the crowd. Strangely, the seats on either side of him were empty even though the auditorium was overcrowded.

Landon Perry was on a stool in the middle of the stage, and he spoke so quietly that everyone in the audience had to lean forward to hear him. Everett, who was the most eager to hear what Landon was saying, could not hear more than a whisper from the astronaut, and as he leaned forward more and more, he fell out of his chair into an infinite abyss. As he fell and fell, images of his mother and his childhood flashed before him. His mother whispered something to him in his dream just as he jolted awake.

When he sat up, his heart was racing and he felt disoriented. It took him a while to take in the features of his room and to bring his awareness out of the dream and realize that none of the events in it had really happened. His dreams were vivid because of his IMAGINATIONAL OVEREXCITABILITY, and he experienced them as though they were real. He would also retain the images and emotions from the dream for a long time.

Shaking, he remembered the managing strategy that he had learned in his ORIENTATION and grabbed his SKEtch pad. He had created a dream journal after they had learned about the OE, and he opened a new page in his journal with his heart still thumping in his throat.

Catching his breath, he created a chart with two columns and titled the columns *things that make sense* and *things that do not make sense*. He noted that it made sense that he was in an auditorium with his classmates to listen to Landon Perry since the astronaut was scheduled to present at the SFGP, but it did not make sense that Landon was elderly and that no one could hear him. The abyss also went into the category for not making sense, but the images of his childhood went into the makes sense category, for although the presentation had been strange, all of the information had been accurate.

He struggled to remember what his mother had whispered to him at the very end of his dream, but it seemed that the harder he tried to concentrate on it, the more the sound of her voice drifted away from him.

Frustrated and disturbed by the dream, he paced around his room for a few minutes and then decided that he wanted to climb the climbing structure in the rec center. He was not sure if it would even be open this late at night, but he left his room and headed for the rec center anyway.

It felt strange to walk through the halls of the school when it was totally quiet, and for a moment, he had the strange feeling that he was still dreaming. He was relieved to see that the rec center was open, and empty, and carefully picked his way to the climbing structure. He stopped for a moment to stare at the sky and took in the stars and the cool night air with all of his senses.

Invigorated, he went to the farthest corner of the structure and started working his way to the top. At first, his muscles protested, still tight from the fright that he had experienced from his dream, but they slowly began to unwind, and he reached out and pulled himself upward with greater and greater agility. With his blood pumping and his eyes focused on finding the next handhold, Everett was able to get rid of the strange feelings that had washed through his body since the dream, and he spent nearly half an hour focusing on the physical exertion and nothing more. He only stopped when his hands reached out for another handhold and found that there were no more.

He had mastered the monolith.

A sense of vertigo washed over him as he lifted himself over the edge and stood up. As he stretched his arms out and lifted his face, he felt like his body was more in the sky than a part of the earth. The climbing structure was three stories high, and he found himself surrounded on all sides by stars and moonlight. There had never been a space for him to go outside at night in the apartment that he had shared with his mother. The beauty and wonder of the moment caused tears to course down his cheeks, although he did not realize that he was crying.

There was no measure of time at the top of the monolith, and Everett was lost in the beauty of the experience for over an hour, although he would later think that it had only been a few minutes. He sighed when he realized that he should go back to his room and slowly worked his way back down the structure.

Just as his feet hit the platform at the bottom, he remembered what his mother had whispered in his dream.

Your father cannot be with us any longer, but he would be very proud of his son.

Shaken by his mother's words and not ready to think about how they fit into his dream, Everett slowly walked away from the climbing structure to leave the rec center and head back to his room. Not paying attention to his surroundings, he nearly walked into another student and jumped back when he realized that someone was standing just in front of him. An apology sprang to his lips, until he realized that the tall red-haired girl standing at the railing was Diedre, the leader of the bullies that called themselves the *originals*.

She turned her head slowly to look at him, and he saw that her cheeks were wet with tears that had just been shed. It made him conscious that his own cheeks were wet, and they self-consciously wiped away their tears at the same time.

No words were shared, but they looked at each other for several moments. Diedre was the first to turn away, and he saw her lift her chin slightly as she looked away from him to continue looking at the stars. He bristled at her reaction and strode out of the rec center. For a moment, it had felt as if there was a shared understanding, a mutual sympathy, but Dre's arrogance had kicked in at the end.

As he entered his room, he realized that he still had a few hours left to sleep, so he crawled under the covers, but the emotions that lingered from his dream and his run-in with Diedre made it hard for him to fall asleep. He tried a few of the visualization techniques that he had created during his ORIENTATION, but each image had a link to his mother, and he could not push the emotions about her aside so that he could use them this time.

Searching through his memories for a new image, he finally settled on his experience with the night sky that he'd had on the monolith. He imagined that he was floating in space, completely surrounded by stars. In his visualization, he slowly drifted farther and farther away from the Earth, surrounded only by the deep chill of space and the distant points of light from the stars that were all around him. The image of floating through the infinity of space finally carried him into a light, restless sleep.

Changing Perspectives

Everett woke up the next morning with a clear memory of the events that had happened the night before. Remembering his strange encounter with Dre, he wondered what had caused her to be at the rec center in the middle of the night and what had caused her tears. He shrugged, thinking that it was not the kind of information that she would ever confide in a *transplant* and ordered his morning meal.

After a quick glance at his timeline, he threw on his comfortable clothing and scarfed down his meal, realizing that he was scheduled to be at his first INTENSIVE in less than ten minutes. He reviewed the map of the location for his class and hurried out the door.

He had to go all the way across campus and was already breathless as he hurried through the lobby. Everett followed the signs to the Arts complex and reached the Dramatic Arts room winded and worried that he was late. The instructor smiled at him as he entered, which reassured him that he had gotten there with time to spare.

Everett found an empty space across the room next to a tall, muscular boy with rich chocolate skin and striking, dark eyes. The other boy looked serious, but gave Everett a brief smile as he settled next to him. Shyly, Everett introduced himself to the older boy and was rewarded with a brief nod and his name, Tobias. Most of the other children had pressed themselves against the walls around the room and looked unsure. A confident trio of boys sat cross-legged in the center of the room, softly laughing and joking with one another. One of them was an *original* that Everett recognized, and he assumed that the others were as well.

He threw his shoulders back and took a deep breath as he told himself that having *originals* in the room would not mar his experience. He perked up when the teacher clapped her hands to get everyone's attention. She calmly invited the children along the walls to join the boys on the floor. Reluctantly, the students detached themselves from the walls and settled into a rough semi-circle. Everett felt a surge of relief when Tobias sat next to him and gave the older boy a brief smile of thanks.

"Good morning!" the instructor said, sweeping the room with a welcoming smile. "I see that I have some students that were assigned to this INTENSIVE and some that elected to take it. I welcome you all. This morning we will talk about how to select a *feature* to imitate. A feature can be a particular walk or body movement, a tone, a type of speech, or an expression. We will start out with big features and work our way down to more subtle ones. Let's try one together."

She gestured at the north wall, and a video clip of a baby playing with blocks appeared. The baby laughed and gurgled as he alternated between banging the blocks together and putting them in his mouth. As the clip ended, the teacher turned back to the group with a smile.

"The easiest feature to imitate is the baby's posture. Show me with your body how the baby was sitting," she said encouragingly.

It took some reassuring nods and statements from the instructor and a great deal of shifting for all of the students to imitate the baby's pose. Everett felt embarrassed at first, but quickly blocked out any worries about what others would think of him when he realized that they were all taking the same risk and thought about how the baby had been sitting. He moved his legs out so that his knees and the sides of his feet touched the floor and widened his arms out in front of him. He felt a little silly, until he got a nod of approval from the instructor.

She helped a few students arrange their bodies to look more like the baby and then gave the room an appreciative nod. After replaying the clip, she directed the class to imitate the feature of the baby's movements. Everett widened his palms to pretend that each hand held a block and then brought them together in the clumsy, joyous way that the baby had. He even pretended to bite on the imaginary blocks a few times and almost felt the drool that should be on his chin.

"Wonderful!" the instructor cried. "You have all been able to transform your movements to look like the baby. Now, I want you to work on something more subtle. I want you to transform just your face. Your expression should match the features of the baby, but the challenge is to transform your face *without* moving your body."

A few nervous murmurs filled the room as the instructor passed out mirrors for each child to practice with. Everett felt nervous and unsure until he saw the instructor praise the *original* for his expression, which spurred Everett to focus on perfecting his own expression. He thought about the baby's look of pure enjoyment, and the muscles in his face slowly relaxed. His eyes widened and brightened, and his mouth and cheeks spread into a smile of eager delight.

The instructor tapped him on the shoulder and nodded to express her approval of him before she moved on to help another student. Everett could not help but look at the *original* as she walked away, and he noted that the other boy's eyes narrowed as he looked back.

It took a while for the instructor to help everyone make the transformation, but she finally gave the group their final challenge.

"Now I would like for you to transform one last thing… your eyes. Your eyes must convey the same emotion as the baby. You cannot use your body or your face… only your eyes," she said softly.

Everett turned back to his mirror and stared vacantly at himself for a while before he jolted himself into trying to change the expression in his eyes. He realized that, unlike the changes that he was able to make with his body, transforming his eyes would have to be more than an imitation. Instinctively, he knew that he would have to reach deep within himself to find the emotion that he wanted to express with his eyes.

Many memories filtered through him, but at last, he found the emotion of pure delight buried deep within and slowly pulled it forward to shine through his eyes. He only saw it for a moment, but he knew that he had done it, and the look of pure delight changed into pride. The instructor walked around to collect the mirrors and asked everyone to stand. She looked into his eyes as he stood up, and her brow furrowed for a moment as she considered him before moving on.

They continued to work on similar activities for the rest of the day, sometimes alone, sometimes with partners, and once with a small group. Everett was fascinated with the amount of control and creativity that was required to complete each activity, and he was thankful that Mr. Dodd had seen the POTENTIAL in him to develop this STRENGTH.

He nodded goodbye to his new friend Tobias when the class was dismissed. The tall boy had shown an incredible range in his performances throughout the day, and Everett felt a deep admiration for his talent. He hoped that he would get to see him again, although he had felt too unsure of himself to make the offer.

A strange feeling washed over him as he faced the hallway that led back to his dormitory. He suddenly felt that he did not want to be locked in his room with the strange emotions from the night before still coursing through him. As he was about to leave, he remembered that CiCi and Sonniy had both been assigned to a sculpture INTENSIVE. Assuming that they would be in the Arts Wing, he turned on his heel to find them. He remembered that Greta should be in the Arts Wing as well, but he knew that she would be hesitant to linger.

It was not difficult to find his friends because they had stayed behind to admire each other's sculptures. Sonniy had tried to sculpt a parrot with its wings folded in, and she was complaining to CiCi that she had only been able to construct the basic form. Each time that she had tried to carve out details like eyes and feathers, they had been uneven, and she'd had to smooth the clay back and start over.

"I think that having the basic form with no details makes it more interesting," CiCi said with a shrug. "I like things that hint at something, instead of having everything exact. It leaves more for people to imagine."

Everett rocked back on his heels, thinking that it was quite an extraordinary statement, and decided to think more about what CiCi had said later. Sonniy dismissed CiCi's insightful statement with a flick of her wrist. She liked things to be exact, realistic, and flawless. The featherless parrot would haunt her for weeks.

They moved over to look at CiCi's sculpture. She proudly hopped onto the stool next to it and balanced precariously on her knees as she gestured to her creation.

"I was trying to create an image of happiness," she explained, cocking her head to one side as she considered her creation.

Her sculpture was a piece of clay that had been stretched and thinned and pulled into a flowing, undulating wave. It somehow had movement and stillness at the same time. Everett was deeply moved and impressed by her work.

Sonniy smiled politely, but Everett got the feeling that she did not understand the meaning behind the abstract sculpture.

Impressed again by the feelings that CiCi was able to make the viewers of her art feel, Everett impulsively gave her a quick hug around the shoulders. She was pleased by his gesture and slipped her hand into his as they turned to walk out of the studio.

She told him that the instructor had mentioned that she could glaze her sculpture later because she had not finished it, and she was thinking about how to color it. As they discussed some possibilities, Sonniy politely interrupted their conversation to invite them to watch her play the cello. They were right down the hall from her practice studio, and she said that she needed to practice anyway.

CiCi politely declined, saying that she had too much work to do back in her room, but earnestly thanked Sonniy for the invitation and reassured her that she would sit in on a practice session sometime that week. Everett eagerly accepted Sonniy's invitation. Watching her would be a great distraction, and he really wanted to know what it was like to play an instrument. He waved goodbye to his young friend as she skipped back toward her dormitory and followed Sonniy to her practice studio.

As they entered, he saw a beautiful wooden instrument resting on a stand with a stool just behind it. The instrument was bathed in a soft golden light, while the rest of the room was rather dim. Everett instantly felt at ease. Sonniy waved at a sensor, and her sheet music was instantly projected onto the opposite wall. She told Everett that he could sit in the soft padded chair that was in the corner.

Everett sat on the edge of the chair to watch as she began warming up on her instrument. He was fascinated by the swift movement of her hand on the bow and the taut control of the fingers of her other hand as they splayed across the strings. Sonniy's usually cheerful face transformed into a mask of concentration as her fingers moved up and down the strings with precision.

A soft chime rang, and a new sheet of music projected onto the wall as a green light filled the room. A soft smile played across Sonniy's face as she recognized the song, and her smile grew bigger as she played. It was an upbeat, foot-tapping kind of song, and her fingers seemed to fly across the strings. The chime sounded again, and Sonniy's cello began to make a somber, mournful sound as the sheet music changed and a red light filled the room. Sonniy's face became drawn and serious. It seemed that she really *felt* each piece of music.

Once the chime sounded a third time and the music changed again, Everett realized that it must be some kind of speed drill. He grew restless, having imagined that he would be relaxing to the notes of a long, beautiful song. The rapid shift between different types of music was not soothing, although he was extremely impressed by Sonniy's ability to play and with the emotion that she was expressing.

After two more song transitions, he decided to slip out. He was easing out of his chair when the light in the room changed to a soft blue, and the music changed again. This song was different from the others. The notes were long and strong, and Everett found himself sinking back into the chair. He closed his eyes as the chords seemed to grow louder and stronger, and he imagined that they moved through him, vibrating his bones and coursing through his blood. He became so lost in the song that when it ended, he felt the same kind of jolt that he experienced when he woke up from a dream.

Sonniy and her cello slowly came back into focus, and he saw that she looked tired. Thinking back on the power of the song, he realized that it took not just dexterity to play her instrument, but strength as well.

"That was an amazing song Sonniy," he said earnestly. "You played it really well."

"Thank you," she said happily. "I wrote it. Playing my instrument is my STRENGTH, but they identified a weakness in composing my own music. I've been working on composing that song all week."

A strange feeling overcame Everett as he felt that he had somehow just met Sonniy. She had not made much of an impression on him before, although he had enjoyed her company, but hearing the notes that she had put together and seeing her passion for playing them gave him a new insight into who she was.

"Thank you for sharing your song with me Sonniy," he said with a shy smile, and she smiled back.

They chatted for a few minutes before Everett left. The music system sent Sonniy a message, alerting her to a few areas the she needed to improve on, so she said that she needed to stay and practice.

The beauty of CiCi's sculpture and the power of Sonniy's song inspired Everett to return to his own projects, and he practically ran back to his room to work on them.

Everett pulled up his technical writing assignment and mentally switched his audience from Greta to Sonniy. She had found a way to communicate *her* passion to him through her music, and he realized that he had not challenged himself by thinking of Greta as the audience to explain his experiment to, because Greta was already passionate about science. He had to change the way that he wrote to be clear to someone not already familiar with the scientific process.

Excited by the challenge that he had given himself, Everett lost himself in his work. His stomach was grumbling and his mouth was dry by the time that he finished, but he felt energized by what he had accomplished. He knew that this draft of his experiment was much clearer and more focused than the original draft had been. He had justified his reasoning and had simplified and clarified his directions.

Stretching, he looked around his room. He could order a meal and eat in his room, but somehow, it did not feel right to be alone. On a whim, he called Kimin to see if she would join him for a meal, but she did not answer, and neither did Greta.

Somewhat irritated by his inability to contact his friends and feeling restless, he left his room and walked to the dining hall alone. To his surprise, it was overflowing with students. He searched through the crowd for his friends but did not see even one of them.

Disappointed, he was about to turn back to his room when he saw that someone was waving at him. Squinting, he realized that it was Tobias, and a huge grin split his face. He waved back and then went to a terminal to secure a hearty meal and a tall, cool glass of lemon water.

He hurried over to Tobias and sat down. The tall boy's dark eyes searched his face with a wry smile before he introduced Everett to the two boys that were sitting with him.

"These are my friends, Anton and Caspan. They have been at the SFGP with me since our ORIENTATION week four years ago," Tobias explained in his deep, rich voice.

The other boys nodded and shook Everett's hand. They were all much taller than Everett, although they did not appear to be the same ages. Caspan was the smallest of the trio and held himself in a quiet, serious way that reminded Everett of Greta. He had light brown skin and large brown eyes. Anton looked slightly younger than Tobias and instantly put Everett at ease with the friendly twinkle that shone in his bright blue eyes.

The trio had already finished eating and were lingering at the table to sip their drinks and chat. Everett mostly ate and drank and added little to the conversation, but he had such an admiration for Tobias and Anton that he felt almost grand sitting with them. They were so strong and sure about what they said.

They were opinionated and disagreed often. Both made articulate points, and as their debates swirled around him, Everett was never able to declare a clear winner. He was impressed by how composed their arguments were and by the confidence with which they delivered them.

It surprised him to notice that although Caspan rarely interjected his opinion, when he did, the older boys immediately grew silent and really considered his words. They did not always agree with him, but it was apparent that they respected and valued his ideas.

"So what are your strength areas?" Caspan finally asked Everett. It was the first time that he had spoken to Everett directly, and his inquisitive brown eyes pierced Everett as he waited for a response.

Everett choked a little on the last bite that he had taken, but he was helped by a generous slap on the back from Anton before he answered, "I have a GENERAL ACADEMIC APTITUDE in math and reading and an interest in science."

Caspan nodded and bit his lip as he considered Everett's words.

"You sound like me, except I have an interest in history," he replied.

He spoke in a slow, measured way, as if he considered every word that he said, a contrast to his older friends. Everett found that he liked Caspan very much.

The small group lingered long enough to keep Everett company as he finished eating but politely excused themselves as soon as his plate was empty. Everett made a tentative plan to meet up with them for dinner sometime that week.

As he headed back to his room, feeling a surge of pride at making three new friends, he remembered that he still had to journal about his experience in his first INTENSIVE.

He sat cross-legged on his bed and pulled his SKEtch pad into his lap. He started a new brain bridge and labeled the first topic INTENSIVE. Knowing that he would have a new INTENSIVE every week, he decided to make a different sub-topic for each one.

After adding the title *dramatic expression*, he zoomed in and drew a quick sketch of the activities that he had participated in. He showed himself smiling in each activity to remind himself that he had truly enjoyed the class. Under the sketches, he drew five stars to represent his interest in the class and a checkmark to show that he wanted to sign up for it again.

Everett decided to record his thoughts about the class and pressed the record button on the SKEtch pad.

"The INTENSIVE in dramatic expression was amazing. I am so glad that Mr. Dodd noticed that I was interested in acting. It surprised me that I could do everything so well, since I am usually kind of shy, but I felt like I didn't have to be shy or self-conscious because I was pretending to be someone else. Sometimes, because of my IMAGINATIONAL OE, I used to pretend to be different people when I was at home. Once I read a book about a boy that got lost in the wilderness, so for a week I pretended like I had gathered the food that I was eating and looked over my shoulder while I ate like I was watching out for predators."

He smiled at the recollection. A lump formed in his throat as he remembered that his mother had never laughed at him when he pretended like that. She had even encouraged him to do it and had shared with him that she sometimes pretended to do things the way a character in a book had done them as well.

"So I guess I've always made myself into other people or characters in my imagination, so now I just have to get comfortable doing it in front of an audience," he finished softly and turned off his SKEtch pad.

Just like I used to pretend to be other characters in front of my mother, he thought and then pushed the idea away, the feeling of betrayal once again washing over him like hot acid.

After taking a few deep breaths to calm himself, Everett put his SKEtch pad away and crawled under the covers. Overall, it had been one of the best days that he had experienced at The School for Gifted Potentials so far.

Unsettling News

The next week passed just as quickly for Everett as the first one had. He was learning to juggle assignments, free time, friendships, and projects. The only blight on his week was the growing anticipation over Landon Perry's visit. Even the faculty was talking about it in excited whispers in the hallways and common areas.

Everett's stomach turned every time he heard the astronaut's name. Landon had been Everett's hero, until the night that he had seen a picture of Landon with his mother when she had been a student at The School for Gifted Potentials. He had set a long-term goal for himself to work his way through a large file of videos, articles, and books about Perry, but whenever he tried to set aside the time to look at it, he found himself creating reasons to avoid the task.

Near the end of the week, Everett made an exciting discovery. He had requested to use the seed from a prehistoric plant in his experiment. The original seed had been found frozen in the arctic tundra over a century before, and scientists had been carefully growing and cultivating the plant ever since to keep the prehistoric species alive. Due to the global importance of finding vegetation that would grow on Mars, Everett had been given one of the precious seeds for his experiment even though he was only a child.

Students at the SFGP were respected as intellectual assets and were responsible for many important scientific findings.

Everett was shocked when he pulled up the data from his plant experiment to find that the seed of the prehistoric plant had sprouted. The evidence of a tendril of growth from the seed was so exciting that he immediately called Greta.

"Hey Greta!" he said excitedly as soon as her face appeared on his screen. "I just checked the data from my plant experiment, and the prehistoric seed that I told you about is *growing!*"

~ 39 ~

"Wow! Everett, that is amazing. Are you using potting soil and water to make it grow?" she asked.

"Actually, my earth science teacher helped me create a soil mixture that is similar to soil samples that were sent back from Mars, and I am not giving water to any of the plants since they haven't found any water on Mars," he responded.

"Hmm. Maybe Earth used to have a similar atmosphere and soil composition to Mars in its prehistory," she replied thoughtfully.

"I know! If that is true, it might help narrow down some plants that could grow on Mars!" he replied.

Everett's voice cracked with excitement, and Greta smiled to show that she understood his joy.

"I have to run down to my lab to see my plant. Do you want to go with me?" he asked, hoping that she would join him to see his thrilling discovery.

Greta leaned forward with a smile as if she was about to agree to go, but then her smile faltered and she shook her head no.

"Sorry, Everett, I just got some feedback from my literature instructor, and I need to make some revisions to my essay. I would be happy to hear about it tomorrow at lunch though," she replied with forced brightness. It was obvious that she really wanted to go with him.

Everett swallowed and forced a smile, disappointed that his friend would not be able to go with him.

"Sure Greta. I'll see you at lunch tomorrow," he replied, hiding his disappointment behind a small smile.

He signed off with a regretful wave and noticed that Greta looked as though she regretted her decision before the screen turned black. Greta had begun to spend more and more time away from her friends and always seemed to be working on her assignments.

Although he was sad that Greta was not going to join him, his excitement over the success of his experiment still coursed through him as he raced to his private laboratory. He waved his badge over the sensor at the door in a blurred motion and nearly tumbled inside. Sucking in a deep lungful of air to calm his racing heart and catch his breath, he stopped for a moment as he entered to let his eyes adjust.

The amount of light on Mars differed significantly from that on Earth, and he and Ms. Everlay had collaborated with a specialist from the planetarium to adjust the amount and duration of sunlight that hit the plants in the experiment to simulate a day on the surface of Mars.

After his eyes adjusted, he quickly made his way to the prehistoric flower, test plant number seventeen. He had selected the number seventeen for his most important seed to honor the companion robot that had helped him through his ORIENTATION.

A fragile tendril of green had emerged from beneath the soil and was reaching up toward the dim light. Everett sucked in his breath at the beauty of the discovery and stood looking at it in awe for several moments.

The sound of ringing and the soft flashing of a blue light shook him out of his reverie, and he fumbled around for the *accept* button for a moment before he pushed it.

Ms. Everlay's excited face appeared on the screen.

"Everett, I am so glad that you are checking on your plant. I saw the data an hour ago and wanted to look at the plant, but I have been waiting for you to see it first. Is it okay if I join you in your lab?" she asked eagerly.

"Yes, you can join me," Everett responded, happy to share the moment with someone that was just as excited as he was.

She was there in only a few minutes and appeared to be out of breath as she entered. Leaning over his shoulder to look at the plant, she inhaled sharply with excitement.

Grabbing her SKEtch pad, she pulled up the plant's data and backed into a corner to look at it. She motioned him over excitedly and pointed out that the tendril had emerged at the same time as a tendril from test plant number twelve had appeared.

He had not even noticed plant number twelve when he had pulled up his data. Sharing a grin of anticipation, they quickly moved over to look at it. After reviewing the setup of each plant, they realized that both of the plants were at the back of the room.

"Is the amount of light different in the back of the room?" he wondered out loud, and his instructor nodded at his question and wrote it down. She pulled up the data for plant number twelve, and they discovered that it was a seed from a cold desert shrub.

Excited by both discoveries, they rapidly began making connections between the two plants. Ms. Everlay suggested that they move to her office so that they could have more space to compare the data, and they jogged down the hallway together, pausing only briefly as she swiped her card to gain entry to her office. She activated the left wall of her room, which looked like it had a collection of handwritten notes and photographs tacked up, but the screen cleared when she waved her hand, and Everett realized that her wall was like a giant SKEtch pad.

After tapping a few things on her SKEtch pad, the screen on the wall became a split screen of the data from plants twelve and seventeen. Soil content, humidity, temperature, light, and airflow data appeared for both plants. She showed him how to highlight similarities in the data by touching a word with his finger, and he spent several minutes absorbed in the data, highlighting similarities as he noticed them.

When he finished, he turned around to show her his work and noticed that she was typing on her SKEtch pad. He waited patiently for her to finish, thinking that she must be catching up on some assignment as he worked.

Looking up with a broad smile, she nodded at his work and then waved her hand over the screen, which caused his data to disappear. She tapped a few things on her SKEtch pad and then laughed when she saw the horrified expression on his face.

"Don't worry! I just transferred your work to my SKEtch pad. I've already sent it to you and a few other people that will be interested in your discovery," she reassured him gently.

He swallowed. It felt strange to know that strangers were going to look at his research, although he knew that he should be proud of his experiment.

"Who did you send it to?" he asked curiously as she led him out of her office and back into the hallway.

"Well, I sent it to Dr. Hassleway, who donated the prehistoric seed to us, as well as Dr. Perry of the INTELLEX crew, Professor Rosenthal because one of her MASTERY students is working on a similar project, and Dr. Grey because she sent us the cold desert shrub seed," she replied.

"Dr. Perry and Dr. Grey?" Everett asked with his heart thudding in his throat.

"Yes, you might know him as Landon Perry, the astronaut that everyone is talking about. He is doing his own research on Mars with plants and will no doubt be interested in viewing your experiment when he is here on his upcoming visit. Dr. Grey is currently stationed in Asia, so it is unlikely that you will get to meet her. No one has seen her since she graduated, but she continues to send us information about her discoveries in Asia and reviews our research when we need her to," she replied.

Landon Perry might want to meet me, Everett thought as he waved goodbye to his instructor. A feeling of dread washed over him. *My mother sent me a seed from Asia. Is she in Asia now?*

The thought sent chills down his back. He had imagined her waiting for him back at their apartment. The thought that she had moved on with her life disturbed him greatly. Ms. Everlay said that Camilla sent information about her discoveries in Asia to the school. How could she have? She spent her days away from him working as a chef and could not have had enough time to travel to Asia and back while he was at school.

His mother had never left him overnight. His first night at The School for Gifted Potentials had been the first time that he had ever slept alone.

How did she fool everyone into thinking that she is in Asia?

Fear of Failure

Everett scowled as he walked into his room. Hearing that Landon Perry might want to talk to him in person about his experiment should have overwhelmed him with excitement, but instead he felt angry for a reason that he could not define. He needed to know just how well Perry had known his mother during her stay at the SFGP. What kind of connection did they have? Why were they no longer friends?

Perry's startling connection to his mother had tarnished Everett's excitement over the astronaut, and he knew that he would feel uncomfortable about him until the mystery of his mother's former life had been solved.

After a small dinner, Everett heard the ringing of a video call and accepted it glumly, expecting another assignment from an instructor. To his surprise, he was told that his presence had been requested at a seminar for the following day.

The CHARACTERISTICS of gifted seminar was part of his schedule every day, but this was the first time that he had been assigned to one. It was a flexible time meant for continuing to build each student's understanding of their unique POTENTIAL and gifted CHARACTERISTICS. So far, he had been given the time off to work on his assignments and projects.

He found that he was excited to attend a seminar. The amount of information that he had learned in his ORIENTATION had seemed overwhelming, but now that he'd had time to process it, he realized that there was more about himself that he wanted to understand.

Another ringing startled him, and he pressed the *accept* button expecting one of his friends. Instead, he received a message that told him that he had earned three hours of social time to use at his discretion.

He smiled at the news. He had not used his social time during his first week. It had been difficult to get his evening routine organized, and his friends had also been too busy getting adjusted to meet up anyway.

He wondered if his friends had earned social time as well as he climbed into bed, hoping for a dreamless sleep.

The following day, Everett was nervous as he waited for his first seminar. His technical writing instructor gave him glowing feedback on his revisions, although she also noted several more sections that she wanted him to work on. He also briefly presented the findings from his plant experiment to his life science class, and several students asked questions that gave him ideas that would improve his experiment's design. Greta smiled broadly at her friend's success, giving him a needed surge of confidence as he stood in front of the class.

He had not started an independent project in his earth science class yet. The class was stimulating, and his instructor had given him a list of categories that he could choose from to research, but nothing had interested him yet. Once the plants in his science project had begun to grow, however, he realized that he wanted to research soil composition.

Everett was thinking about his new research project when he passed a group of new students going into the dining hall. His throat constricted as he watched a young boy turn and ask his robot to show him how to use a food terminal. Memories of Sev came rushing back, and he realized how much he missed the robot's companionship each night as he sat alone in his room.

Sighing, he sat down with Kabe and Greta with his meal clutched tightly in his hands. They could not find their other friends but had a relaxing meal together anyway. Greta noticed Kabe nod a hello to Jace and saw it returned.

She leaned in to ask, "So, are you and Jace friendly now?"

Kabe chewed slowly and took several moments to respond.

"He and I talk every once in a while," he finally shared. "We have a lot of the same STRENGTHS and interests. It's a little awkward, though, because Jeremiah gets upset whenever he sees me with Jace. I also don't like the way Jace and his friends treat the *transplants*."

Everett nodded, feeling sympathy for his friend. Everett did not have any cousins that he knew of, but he imagined that it must be difficult for Kabe to be torn between his friend and his cousin in that way.

Greta touched Kabe's arm and smiled softly. She nodded at the small group of new students, evident because of their robots, and told Kabe that she had been watching them all week.

"I have noticed a few of the *originals* tormenting them, but I have never seen Jace take part. Maybe he is changing because of you," she offered hopefully.

A strange expression crossed Kabe's face, and he smiled to show Greta that he appreciated the information.

They parted ways after lunch. Kabe headed to the rec center, Greta went back to her room to work on her assignments, and Everett ran down to his lab, eager to check on the progress of his plants.

The rest of his day went quickly, and he walked down the hall with a sense of excitement and trepidation about his first seminar. As he entered the room, tears pricked his eyes when he saw the smiling face of Mr. Dodd.

"Mr. Dodd," he forced out, his voice sounding strangled. "I didn't think that I would see you again!"

Mr. Dodd smiled and chuckled.

"Well, I didn't say anything about seeing you again because there was no guarantee that I would have you in a seminar, but I am glad to see you!" Mr. Dodd said heartily as he clapped Everett on the shoulder.

Tears welled up in Everett's eyes and threatened to spill over. Seeing Mr. Dodd, someone that he had connected deeply with, reminded him of how intense his EMOTIONAL OVEREXCITABILITY was. He bonded deeply with people, and renewing his connection with his kind instructor caused a wave of relief to course through him.

Everett was surprised to see Caspan walk in next. They lit up as they saw each other and gave each other an awkward hello. Another student, an older girl with long, shiny dark hair and glittering black eyes entered next. She smiled when she saw Mr. Dodd but looked at the boys shyly. Caspan introduced himself and Everett in his soft, husky voice, and she smiled faintly.

"My name is Leotie," she told them, raising her chin slightly as she spoke.

To Everett's surprise, Greta walked in next. He grinned and went to her side. Seeing that she looked nervous, he introduced her to Caspan and Leotie. Greta nodded and twisted her hands.

"Welcome, my dear friends," Mr. Dodd said as he asked them all to take a seat.

Everett noticed that there were large cushions and even some hammock swings to sit on, but there were no traditional chairs in the room.

Everett, Greta, and Leotie each dragged a large pillow over to Mr. Dodd's feet, while Caspan headed for a hammock as if he had been to a seminar before.

"Greta, I would like to start by sharing that I noticed that you looked nervous as you walked in," Mr. Dodd said gently. "Do you want to share what you are feeling with us?"

Greta flushed and smoothed her skirt.

"Well, I have not been called into a seminar before, so I am worried that I got invited to one because I have done something wrong," she said in a voice barely above a whisper.

"We don't get called into seminars because we're in trouble," Caspan interjected comfortably from his hammock. "They just invite us to a seminar if they find that there is a

CHARACTERISTIC of giftedness that they think we should know more about. I get invited to seminars all the time."

Caspan swung confidently in the hammock as he spoke, and Greta seemed to relax at his observation.

Mr. Dodd nodded.

"Yes Greta, being called into a seminar is a way for you to develop a deeper understanding of your giftedness. We covered a lot of information during your ORIENTATION, but there is much more about yourself to discover, and each student has different CHARACTERISTICS to learn more about. So with that, I would like to welcome you all. I am here to discuss *goals* with you today."

Everett sat up on his knees when he saw Greta tense up and reached over to squeeze her hand. Leotie looked confused.

"I already set goals during my ORIENTATION and in my classes," Leotie said. "I am already working to complete them. Why are we here to set goals?"

"We are not here to *set* goals," Mr. Dodd replied. "We are here to talk about the feelings and frustrations that sometimes go along with setting and achieving goals. All of you have set goals but are working to complete them in different ways. Greta, why don't you talk about how you feel about the goals that you set?"

She flushed again and twisted her hands. It took her so long to start talking that Everett wanted to jump in and take her place, but he noticed that everyone else was giving her time to start talking, so he sat back with his jaw clenched.

Finally, she said, "I set a long-term goal during my ORIENTATION that I am concerned about completing. As soon as my classes started, I had lots of short-term goals that I set for daily assignments, but I also have some long-term goals that I set for my classes, plus the one that I set during my ORIENTATION. I just feel overwhelmed, and I want to do my best on all of them. As soon as I finish a daily assignment, I start working on my long-term goals."

"So what is your greatest fear about not completing a goal?" Leotie asked softly.

Greta's head snapped to the side to look at the other girl, and she seemed frozen by her question.

"Well, I guess I just want everything to be perfect," she finally answered. "I just want to make sure that it all turns out the way that I pictured it."

Everett nodded at her words. He finally understood why she was always working on assignments. His mouth turned into a thoughtful frown when he realized that he also wanted everything to be perfect, but he did not work all the time like Greta did.

"Everett, it looks like you have something to share," Mr. Dodd said kindly.

"Well, I was just thinking that I am kind of like Greta, because I also want everything that I do to be perfect. I get a picture in my mind of what I want it to be like, but then when it doesn't turn out the right way, instead of working hard on it like Greta, I kind of avoid it," he said.

"That sounds just like me!" Leotie shared excitedly and then clapped her hands over her mouth. She looked embarrassed that she had participated so freely.

"I'm more like Greta," Caspan shared from his swing. "I have more goals than I should probably set, and then I worry and worry about finishing them. I usually complete them ahead of the time that I scheduled, but somehow, that still doesn't feel like it's *enough*. It just makes me want to set *more* goals and work even harder."

Greta sat up eagerly and twisted her neck to look at Caspan.

"Yes! That is just what it feels like for me. I set too many goals and I work like crazy to meet them, but then I'm not satisfied even when I complete them. I have felt that way my whole life. It was never a fear of getting in trouble. All of my projects were driven by me and *my* need to learn. No one ever got mad at me for not doing a perfect job, except me I guess," she said with a frown.

The other children nodded thoughtfully.

"I guess I don't understand why I have the same feelings as Greta, but her feelings make her want to work harder, and mine make me want to do anything but the assignment," Everett finally added. "I avoid it until I absolutely have to get it done and then I get an upset stomach and get mad at myself for not doing it sooner."

Leotie giggled softly as she related to what he was saying.

"Greta, if we were to look at your goal timelines, would you say that you are ahead of schedule on your long-term projects or behind schedule?" Mr. Dodd asked.

Greta looked at the ceiling as if visualizing the timeline on her SKEtch pad.

"I am definitely ahead," she finally said. "Even though I know that I'm ahead of schedule, I worry that something might come up in the future that will set me back, so I try to stay a few steps ahead."

"So instead of using catastrophe thinking and planning around what-ifs, why don't you come up with a plan for handling a catastrophe so that you can relax the rest of the time?" Mr. Dodd suggested.

Greta and Caspan exchanged a look that said that they liked the suggestion.

"Greta, why don't you and Caspan work together to create a plan that will work for you, and I will talk to Everett and Leotie," Mr. Dodd said after seeing the look that they had shared.

Greta nodded and stood up to join Caspan. She stood next to his hammock awkwardly for a moment and smiled when he moved over for her to sit next to him.

"So, Everett and Leotie. It sounds like Greta and Caspan deal with their need to be perfect by working ahead of schedule to be sure that they finish their goals in time, while you deal with the need to be perfect by avoiding the task until the last possible moment and then you work yourselves into a frenzy trying to complete it," Mr. Dodd said, leaning forward to look at them.

Both children nodded slowly.

"Is that the same for all tasks?" he asked, cocking his head to one side.

"Sometimes, if I can get going on a project and I don't think about the goal, I can work on it forever. It seems like I only avoid a task if I feel unsure about the outcome or if I think about the amount of time that I have to do it," Leotie answered.

"I have been avoiding my long-term goal because there is an emotional distraction involved, but I also avoid some of my short-term assignments, like my technical writing homework, because I'm just unsure of what to do and I don't want to get it wrong," Everett added.

"As Leotie asked Greta, what is *your* greatest fear about not completing a goal?" Mr. Dodd asked them with an ironic smile.

They shared a look and shrugged.

"Well, I guess I just want everything to be perfect. I want it all to turn out the way that I pictured it," Leotie answered wryly, aware that she was echoing Greta's sentiments.

Everett nodded to agree.

"So you might need some kind of picture of the end product in mind. You can sketch or write out a plan for what "perfect" will mean to you at the beginning of the project so that you will know what it should look like in the end. That might take away some of your fear, and it will give you something clear to work toward," Mr. Dodd offered.

Everett and Leotie smiled and chatted for a while about how they could apply this strategy to the work that they were currently doing. It seemed like only a few minutes had passed before Mr. Dodd regretfully informed them that their seminar was over.

They stood up awkwardly, not wanting their conversations to end.

"Will you all eat dinner with me?" Caspan asked them. "I'd like to implement part of the plan that I just made with Greta, but if you all don't eat with me, I might be tempted to run back to my room to do some work."

An impish smile crossed his face, and they all laughed when they realized that he was joking. They agreed to eat with him, and each child gave Mr. Dodd a parting hug as they left.

When they got to the cafeteria, Caspan and Everett noticed Anton and Tobias just as Greta noticed Kimin, Sonniy, and Kabe. Anton and Tobias were already seated with their meals, but Kimin, Sonniy, and Kabe had just entered. After an awkward discussion, they all agreed to get their food and sit with Caspan's friends.

As they settled into their seats and introduced themselves, they discovered that Leotie and Kimin already knew each other from an INTENSIVE, which Everett explained was where he had met Tobias. The group ate, talked, and laughed as if they had known one another for years. The conversation drifted from projects, to INTENSIVES, and finally to the rec center. Kabe mentioned to Anton that he and Everett had attempted to climb the three-story structure together but had not reached the summit.

"Would you be interested in a friendly race to the top?" Tobias asked, leaning toward Kabe and Everett with his dark eyes twinkling. A fire lit up Kabe's blue eyes as he responded that he would love a good race. Everett knew that he was the least athletic one of the group, but he also knew that he had reached the top of the monolith once before, so he agreed to race them.

"Let's meet up tomorrow. We can get some work done in the morning, have our race in the afternoon, and still get back to our rooms in time to rest up for our INTENSIVE classes the next day," Anton suggested as the group got up to return to their dormitories.

"Sure," Kabe and Everett responded at the same time.

They all said goodbye, but Everett hung back to talk to Greta alone.

"It was good to find out why you've been so worried about your assignments," he said shyly. "It's funny that we have the same concern, living up to our own high expectations, but we definitely handle it differently. Do you feel better now that you've talked about it?"

She nodded and picked an imaginary piece of lint off of her vest.

"It does feel better," she agreed. "Caspan and I made a plan to check in on each other, and we are going to meet once a week to review each other's goals and talk about our progress on them. We are helping each other stay realistic about our goals and have promised to spend some time away from our assignments."

Everett smiled, hoping that this meant that he would see more of Greta.

"What INTENSIVE are you signed up for?" he asked, wanting to prolong their conversation. She fidgeted, and he could tell that she was trying to fight her impatience to get back to her work.

"I was assigned to a ballet class," she shared with a pleased blush. "I don't know how the instructors are able to read my interests so well. I checked out a flute after my INTENSIVE last week. Sometimes I play the tunes that I learned when I am feeling stressed."

"I enjoyed my INTENSIVE in dramatic expression. I am signed up for a freshwater ecology INTENSIVE. We are going to leave early in the morning to take some samples from a nearby pond and then we will examine the organisms that we find in a lab back here at school," he told her, flushing with excitement.

She squealed uncharacteristically and grabbed his wrists.

"You have to tell me all about it when you get back! If it is as great as it sounds, that will be the first INTENSIVE that I pick to take once we can choose our own," she vowed.

They grinned at each other.

"Do you want to go the Nature Center with me tomorrow?" he asked as they reached her hallway. "I could meet up with you after my race with Kabe."

"Sure," she said shyly and slowly turned on her heel to walk down the hallway to her room.

Everett stared after her, hoping that discussing her need to be perfect in the seminar would help her overcome the fear that her work would be unsatisfactory so that she could spend more time with her friends.

Impatience

The following day, Everett rushed to the rec center to meet up with Anton, Tobias, and Kabe for their friendly race to the top of the monolith. He stretched his arms as he ran and thought about which pathway he would take. He had climbed to the top of it once, on a night that he would never forget, but he had been fueled by frustration and had not been competing against anyone but himself. Now he was a ball of nervous energy, and he knew that this climbing experience would be different.

Tobias and Anton were there when he arrived, and the boys exchanged a few playful challenges with one another as they waited for Kabe to show up. He sauntered over to the group with his confident smile, and the joking ceased.

The boys sized one another up for a moment before Tobias cleared his throat.

"Anton and I have been at the SFGP a lot longer than you guys and have already spent a lot of time climbing this. We agreed to give you guys a head start," he said.

Kabe's eyes darkened.

"I agreed to this race because I want a challenge, not because I want you to let me win," he told the teens, sounding offended.

Their faces changed as they processed what he said, and Everett saw a look of respect cross their eyes. He swallowed, thinking that he had been about to accept the advantage. It was hard not to admire Kabe for his drive and motivation.

The boys spread out so that they each had a different starting location, and after a brief countdown, they propelled themselves forward. Everett was immediately in last place. He had started at a spot that had ropes and did not get a good grip on the rope to heft himself up.

Looking up, he saw that Kabe and Tobias were in the lead, with Anton not far behind. Everett knew that he would not win, but he took Kabe's words to heart and decided to look at it as a challenge. If he put forth the effort and made it to the top, he would be proud of himself, but he also knew that his competitive spirit would make him come back and practice. He would not give up on winning the race someday.

Everett pulled himself up one handhold at a time. When he was about halfway up, he heard a shout of joy and looked up to see Tobias standing triumphant at the top of the monolith. Everett was glad that the older boy had respected Kabe's request for a challenge and had truly put forth his best effort. Despite that, it was only a few moments before Kabe joined him at the top. A reckless smile of pride cracked Kabe's face before he bent forward with his hands on his knees to catch his breath.

Anton joined them at the top after a few minutes had passed. Everett continued to pull himself up and concentrated on getting to the top. When he reached out for the very last handhold, he was startled when he felt strong hands gripping his forearms. He looked up in surprise and saw Tobias's grinning face above him.

He allowed his friend to pull him up to the top of the climbing structure and found that his limbs were quivering. He put his hands on his knees and bent forward, struggling to catch his breath, and hoped that the others would not notice the shaking of his limbs.

When he did look up, he was surprised that all three boys were looking at him with respect in their eyes.

Anton slapped him on the shoulder and said, "Most people would have given up when they knew that they would be last, but you stuck with it. That's pretty respectable."

Everett grinned and punched the other boy playfully on the arm before he turned to look out at the view. At night, he had been surrounded by a world of stars. Now he could see the land around the school as it stretched for several miles. He was surprised to see an entire village of tents set up on the west lawn.

He pointed it out to Kabe, who said, "They are preparing that space for Landon Perry. They will be hosting special dinners and presentations out there once he arrives."

Everett sighed. It seemed that he could not get away from news about the astronaut.

Silently, the small group sat down to rest with their legs swinging over the side of the climbing structure. A sudden flurry of activity around the tents caught their attention, and they watched with interest as the Chancellor strode up to the largest tent to inspect it. He was far away, but Everett would recognize him anywhere.

Three people stood behind him, and Everett was surprised when he realized that they were wearing the student uniform. He caught the glimmer of red hair and knew that he was looking at Dre. He thought that maybe the tall, blond boy next to her was Jace, and his eyes flicked to Kabe to see if he had noticed. Kabe was watching the scene with narrowed eyes, and Everett assumed that the other boy had noticed his cousin.

There was a lot of gesturing between the Chancellor and the person in charge of the tent's construction. Finally, the large group walked into the tent. Everett and his friends watched for a while, waiting to see if they would come out, but Anton and Tobias stood up after several minutes had passed. They said that they had to get back to work, but wanted to set up a weekly race. Kabe and Everett stood up as well and eagerly agreed to make it a regular event.

Tobias and Anton went down first, and after another glance at the tent, Everett and Kabe followed.

Everett waved goodbye to Kabe as he turned to walk over to the Nature Center. Greta was not there yet, and he was not sure if he should go in without her or wait for her outside. Due to the extreme cold on the inside, he decided to wait for her at the entrance and paced around the entryway, scanning the rec center while he waited for her to arrive. For a moment, he worried that she had forgotten about their plan, or that she had changed her mind about coming, until he realized that no matter what her worries were about her assignments, she had never let him down before.

His head snapped up when he heard his name, and he saw Greta running toward him. A grin of relief covered his face, and she squeezed his forearms in a breathless hello when she reached him. She apologized for being late, and he filled her in on the race and the village of tents that they had seen from the roof as they hurriedly put on their protective gear.

"Wow, I'm impressed that you made it all the way up," she acknowledged as she zipped up her coat. "Sometimes I get that kind of motivation, like it just comes from nowhere, or from somewhere deep inside of me, and I can do things that I never thought were possible, like completely finishing my first long-term goal this morning."

A shy grin of pride covered her face as she acknowledged her accomplishment. Everett hugged her around the shoulders as he pulled her deeper into the Nature Center.

"Well. With an achievement like that, I guess we should celebrate," he said.

Their shared laugh echoed happily across the frigid plains.

The following day, Everett rushed through the lobby of the SFGP to meet the instructor of his INTENSIVE and was surprised to see the weathered face of Ms. Rosenthal in the doorway. She looked him over with a wry smile as she announced to the group that the last student had arrived and that they could now board the PODs that would take them to their INTENSIVE.

Everett flushed with embarrassment over being late as the other students pushed through the doors of the school and got in line for a POD. A momentary sense of alarm swept over him as he stepped into the fresh air outside of the school. He pushed out his pent-up breath and realized that he had felt like a prisoner at the school.

Could it really be this easy? Was it possible for a student to just walk out, get in a POD, and find their way home? He was not sure. Maybe they had only released him because he was with an instructor.

Ms. Rosenthal was suddenly in front of him, staring quizzically at him.

"You still haven't made up your mind about this place, have you?" she asked.

He remembered how angry he had been the day that he met her during his ORIENTATION, how sure he had been that he did not belong at The School for Gifted Potentials.

He swallowed, knowing that he did not feel the same way about the school anymore, but he did not want to admit that to her.

"I guess not," he said, squinting up at her, and was surprised when she answered him with a grin.

"Then I guess you and I have something in common," she said and ducked into a waiting POD with a smirk.

Everett was glad that he did not have a chance to answer her as he got into his own unoccupied POD. Her response mystified him, but he assumed that she had said it just to throw him off balance. It was hard to believe that an instructor did not like The School for Gifted Potentials.

As the car raced forward, he leaned back in his seat, trying not to think about his last trip in a POD, the one that had brought him to the SFGP. Instead, he forced his mind to drift to his first seminar. He had learned a lot about himself in the seminar. He had never made the connection that he and Greta shared the CHARACTERISTIC of wanting to be perfect because they handled the feeling so differently. He was also glad that it had helped him become closer to Caspan. Most of all, it had given him the chance to see Mr. Dodd again. Somehow, knowing that his favorite instructor might appear in his life periodically, although unpredictably, gave Everett a sense of stability that had been lacking for him.

You still haven't made up your mind about this place, have you?

He thought about Ms. Rosenthal's question. When he had met her, he would have done anything to get away from The School for Gifted Potentials. His friends and his classes had changed his mind about the school, or so he had thought. If that was true, why had he felt such a sense of relief when he had stepped out of the doors to the school and into the open air? He knew that part of the reason was because he felt trapped, partly by the Chancellor, but also partly by the feeling that he no longer had anywhere to escape to.

If he saw his mother again, what would he say to her? What life was she living now that she had left him behind? With all that he had learned about her, it was difficult to imagine that she was still in their apartment, going to her job as a chef each day. Was she in Asia, as Ms. Everlay had said?

He rolled his head around on his neck to relieve the tension that these questions always stirred up. Although he was angry with his mother, his EMOTIONAL OE caused him to continue to feel a deep connection to her. It also caused the feelings of betrayal and confusion to continue to sting like the first time that he had experienced them, and his stomach dropped each time that he thought about her. After taking a few deep breaths, his stomach started to unclench, and he turned his attention to the scenery that was racing by outside his window.

He had always felt a deep sense of peace when he was exploring in nature. The kaleidoscope of thoughts and ideas that usually ran through his mind seemed to still when he was outside, and he was able to drift and just take in the world around him with all of his senses. That thought reminded him to take his noise reduction implements out so that he could enjoy all of the sounds of nature once he was out of the POD. He had been plagued by daily irritation from sounds his entire life, until he was given the set of sound filters at The School for Gifted Potentials. They helped him tune out distracting sounds so that he could focus on what he needed to learn.

In fact, the school had helped him address many of the issues that he experienced due to his SENSUAL OE. The lighting had been adjusted in his room, and he had selected smoother sheets for his bed. Not only did the school give him options for ways to *cope* with his SENSUAL OE, it also gave him plenty of opportunities to enjoy it.

He squirmed in his seat as he realized that he had not set aside any time to participate in the activities that the school offered for those that needed to enjoy sensory experiences. A video message was sent to him each evening that informed him of the events that were happening, but he was still too overwhelmed with juggling his assignments and making time for his friends to participate in them.

Everett sighed, knowing that there was more to The School for Gifted Potentials than he had even had time to experience. It was an uncomfortable reminder that the school really did meet all of his needs, except for his need to be with his mother.

Everett entered his room thinking only about taking a long, cleansing shower. He had hiked up the side of a mountain, collected multiple samples of pond water from targeted sections of water along the bank, and had even rowed to the center of the pond to take samples from three different depths. He and the other students had carried the samples and the equipment back down the mountain, and the exertion of that climb, in addition to climbing the monolith the day before, had left his muscles a little shaky.

As he walked in, he noticed that his screen was blinking and pressed the *accept* button as he wondered who the message was from.

The MASTERY student that was working with Everett at the planetarium appeared.

"Good evening Everett. I am sending this message to inform you that you have completed the two week elective that your advisor selected for you. You may decide to continue your work at the planetarium, or you can choose a new elective. Please let me know what your decision is when you join me at the planetarium tomorrow."

With a brief smile, he was gone. Everett was surprised. Two weeks had gone by faster than he had thought possible. The hour that he spent each day in the planetarium was amazing, and he knew that he had not even scratched the surface of possibilities for study in the planetarium yet. Despite that, he was curious to find out what else he could do as an elective.

I should ask my friends what their electives are so that I can see what other options are available, he thought.

He called Greta first. Their interests were similar, so he was curious to find out what her elective was. Out of all of his friends, her elective would probably tempt him to switch the most. He was surprised that they had never discussed it, but then, it seemed like they had not found the time to have a long conversation since they had met. There was always something to do or somewhere to be.

She was not in her room to accept his call, so he left her a message to call him as soon as she returned.

Shrugging, he called Kabe next.

"Hey Kabe. My elective is almost over, unless I want to continue studying at the planetarium, so I was wondering what other options there are for me to choose from. What is your elective?" he asked.

Kabe smiled as he responded, "I am working with a MASTERY student that studies industrial architecture. He is teaching me the basic structures of bridges right now, so there is no way that I'm going to change my elective this soon. Does that sound interesting to you?"

Everett frowned. "It does sound really interesting, but I'm not sure that it matches any of my STRENGTHS. I'll keep that in mind for when we are allowed to pick our own INTENSIVES though. Thanks."

Kabe nodded and the screen went black.

That is an interesting elective. I wonder what else is available, Everett thought as he called Kimin.

"Hey Everett!" Kimin squealed when she saw his face. "What's with the frown?"

Everett flushed. He had not realized that he was frowning.

"Hey Kimin. I am just calling around to find out what everyone is doing for their elective," he said quickly.

"Oh okay. I'm working with the toddlers. I get to help them with learning by discovery, I talk to them to help them develop their language skills, and I even designed a lesson for them yesterday. I love it! I don't think that I'm going to change my elective for a while," she said with a soft smile.

It was obvious that her advisor had picked the right elective for her.

"That sounds really great Kimin. Thanks for letting me know," he said.

They signed off with a wave.

He made a few more calls and found out that Jeremiah was studying the number pi, Sonniy was working with a MASTERY student studying solar power, and CiCi was learning how to draw using different perspectives. As he signed off from his last call, he rocked back in his chair, amazed at the diverse interests and STRENGTHS of his friends. He frowned when he realized that he had still not heard back from Greta.

Sighing, he turned on his SKEtch pad to look at his plant data. There was nothing new to report, although he was pleased that his plants continued to grow slowly, so he pulled up his timeline to review his goals. His stomach twisted as he looked at his long-term goal, *finish the Landon Perry file*.

For a moment, he considered opening the Landon Perry file. Maybe if he read more of the autobiography, especially the chapters that told about Perry's years as a student at the SFGP, Everett would get more insight into the astronaut's relationship with his mother. It was possible that she was even mentioned in the book.

Just as he was about to click on the file, however, he was overcome by an intense feeling of anger. He grimaced and tossed the SKEtch pad onto his bed. He pushed himself off of his chair and paced around his room. Deep breathing and movement settled his emotions somewhat, but he was unable to sit down and do his assignments with the conflicting feelings of curiosity and anger still rolling through him. He glanced at his screen, hoping that Greta would call him back.

Impatient for her to call and too upset to work, he decided to take the shower that he had forgotten about to distract himself from his feelings.

As he stepped into the shower, he realized that none of his friends were considering changing their electives yet. Why was *he* so impatient? He loved what he was learning at the planetarium, and outer space had always fascinated him. It was disconcerting that his friends could all stick to things longer than he could. He shook his head. He knew that the INTELLECTUAL OVEREXCITABILITY could create the need to learn many things at once, but it also created a drive to stay with one topic of study for many years.

He frowned.

Maybe it's not that I'm impatient to finish my study at the planetarium. Maybe it's that I'm still so upset that my mother left me here, that I found out that she lied to me about who I am, and that now I don't feel like I fit anywhere.

Of course he liked attending The School for Gifted Potentials. He was excited about what he was learning, he felt great about the friends that he had made, and he enjoyed having control over what he learned. He just… he just needed his mother to help him through the journey. He still needed to have her to depend on. Losing his trust in his mother had left a gaping hole in him that he was not sure he could ever fill, no matter how many different classes he took or how many friends he made.

Everett sighed as he climbed out of the shower and rolled his shoulders around to release the tension that had built with his pensive musing. He closed his eyes for a moment and breathed deeply.

Think about what you can control, he told himself firmly.

After an internal struggle, he felt his emotions settle. He breathed calmly, slowly got dressed, and looked himself in the eye through the mirror for a long moment before heading back into his room.

The smooth textiles of his sleeping clothes cooled Everett's pink skin as he walked back into his room, and he noticed that a new message was waiting for him. Thinking that it was probably Greta returning his call, he eagerly pushed *accept*.

It was not Greta's face that greeted him.

Landon Perry's smiling face was on his screen.

"Good evening Everett. I was informed that you made a significant discovery about two plant species that might grow on Mars. I look forward to hearing more about your work on my upcoming visit to the SFGP. Thank you for your innovative work on this important area of study."

It was a brief message, but it left Everett feeling breathless. The small measure of control that he had managed to pull together crumbled. Without thinking, he stumbled out of his room and walked around the nearly empty hallways for almost an hour. A few students looked curiously at him as they crossed paths. They were still dressed in uniforms, and he was in his sleeping clothes, but he was too distracted by his emotions to even notice them.

Receiving a personal message from Landon Perry distressed him. It was no longer just a possibility that he would be face to face with someone that had known his mother when she had attended this school, someone that he suspected had known her very well. Landon had confirmed that he would seek Everett out.

What would Everett say to him?

How could he ask him the questions that were constantly on his mind?

Somehow, he ended up in the hallway that lead to the Life and Natural Sciences Wing and stood in front of the photograph of his mother and Landon at the groundbreaking ceremony. Landon's strong profile and shining eyes dominated the photograph. Everett's mother was next to him, clinging to his arm, her pretty face almost covered by her long hair. He had not recognized her the first time that he had seen the picture, but then, he could not have expected to see a picture of her hanging on a wall at the SFGP at that time.

My mother told me that my father passed away. Landon Perry cannot be my father.

But then, she had lied about everything else.

Her name.

Her history.

Why couldn't he face that she could have lied about his father as well?

Everett sat down under the picture for a long time, letting his thoughts and emotions drift.

What did Landon have to do with his mother?

Was he Everett's father?

Was he the reason that she had wanted to keep him away from this school?

If Landon *was* his father, why wouldn't she have told him that? Knowing that one of the most famous astronauts in the world was his father would have been an incredible thing to know as he grew up. He would have followed the news about INTELLEX crew; he would have paid more attention to Landon's interviews.

If Landon Perry was Everett's father, did he know that he had a son?

If he did, why had he never contacted Everett?

Choosing Sides

Everett was distracted as he walked into his life science class the next day. He had slept very little after receiving Perry's call and had not finished any of his assignments. Worry gnawed at his tired mind, and he barely smiled at Greta as he slid into the seat next to her.

"Hello," she said, cocking her head to the side when she sensed that he was not his usual self.

He grimaced and then asked, "Why didn't you return my call last night?"

His tone was more accusatory than he had intended, and she flushed.

"I'm sorry. Kimin had already arranged to meet up with me for a late meal, so I was frantically working to complete my assignments before we had to get together. She is having trouble with some of the *originals*, and she wanted my advice," she said apologetically.

He squeezed her wrist gently.

"That's okay," he replied with a kinder tone. "I just wanted to know what elective you are taking. I have the option of changing mine today, so I was curious to know what other options there are."

"Oh, I am studying biomimicry. The MASTERY student that I'm working with looks at problems that humans have, or needs that humans have, and then looks at how animals and plants solve those problems. Then she designs a product that humans can use that makes the problem go away," she replied, spreading her hands apart to make it look like something had just disappeared. "I'm not going to change my elective yet. I still have so much to learn. I am even starting to get some ideas of my own."

He nodded with a sigh. If all of his friends were able to dedicate themselves to one area of learning for more than two weeks, he felt like he should continue his studies as well.

I need to work through my impatience and stick with my elective at least one more week, he decided.

His instructor breezed into the classroom and quickly got the class started on creating an experimental design. After everyone was working quietly in small groups, she pulled Everett aside.

"I got an exciting message last night," she said softly. "Landon Perry would like to meet with you about your experiment! I will be in touch with you about your experimental design so that you will know how to answer his questions. I would like to share the news with your class. Would that be okay?"

His stomach dropped. Imagining all of their eyes turning to look at him, wondering what they were thinking, having to answer all of their questions...

"Sorry, but I just don't feel comfortable sharing that with the class right now," he responded quietly.

He avoided her eyes, thinking that his choice would disappoint her, but she squeezed his hand and smiled warmly at him.

"Of course. Just let me know if you change your mind," she said encouragingly and left his side to assist a group that had a question.

Greta looked at him quizzically when he returned to their group, but he just smiled uncomfortably and avoided her inquisitive eyes for the rest of the class period.

Everett walked to the dining hall later that day with his shoulders drooping. Landon Perry's imminent visit had put a damper on Everett's discovery of the prehistoric plant because it meant a private meeting with the astronaut. Everett was not sure if he would be able to talk to him about the experiment without shouting out what he really wanted to know.

What do you know about my mother? Everett imagined asking him over and over in his mind.

He ran into Caspan when he stopped at a food terminal to grab a quick lunch. After a quick chat about how their days were going, they both expressed a desire to spend some time in the rec center. They both ordered a sandwich to eat as they walked down the hall together. As they walked in companionable silence, Everett spotted Dre walking toward them from the opposite direction. She was laughing loudly with her arm linked through the arm of a dark haired girl that was about the same height. Her face froze for a moment when she spotted Everett and then she and her companion were gone.

Caspan looked at Everett from the corner of his eye.

"Do you know Diedre?" he asked, sounding surprised.

"Oh, no, I mean not really," Everett stammered. "She bullied me a little when I got here. I guess she still remembers me."

"Yeah, she does that to all the new students. I think it's because she doesn't trust that she should really be here, so she tries to make everyone else feel like they don't," Caspan observed casually.

Everett was amazed by his friend's remark. He had never thought about Dre bullying other kids because she was insecure. It had always seemed like she despised the new kids because she believed that she was better than they were, but it made sense that it could be the opposite. Mr. Dodd had said that the students that started as babies had been tested just as thoroughly as the students that started as children, but maybe Dre did not really trust that. His friend's theory definitely gave him another way to look at the *original's* behavior.

Caspan and Everett split up with a friendly wave as they entered the rec center.

Everett scanned the room, looking for a new activity to grab his attention, and was startled when he saw Kabe playing a game with Jace. They were passing a flying disk between them from opposite edges of a court of some kind. Each time that they caught the disk, a pattern of colored lights would flash across it. Sometimes it seemed as though Jace was triumphant, and other times Kabe seemed to have the advantage. Everett could not figure out what the flashing patterns meant and shrugged.

As he turned on his heel to find an activity, he bumped into Jeremiah. Everett realized that Jeremiah had been watching the cousins play with a scowl on his face. He looked down at Everett sadly as he turned to follow him away from the court.

"Hey Everett. I haven't seen you very much lately. It seems like Kimin is the only one that ever calls me to do anything," Jeremiah said with a bitter glance over his shoulder at Kabe and Jace.

"I'm really sorry Jeremiah. I just haven't had much time to get together with anyone," Everett said sheepishly. He had not had much time for anyone, except for Greta, and he did not feel like he had spent much time with her either.

Jeremiah shrugged and shoved his hands into his pockets.

"That's okay. I know that everyone is busy. It's just… well I guess I just thought that we were all such great friends during our ORIENTATION, and it seems like we've drifted apart a little," Jeremiah shared.

Everett nodded thoughtfully.

"I guess so. I just think that we are all really busy getting to know our schedules and learning how to get all of our work done. It might take a while for us to get into a routine that will let us spend more time together," he told Jeremiah, hoping to reassure him.

Everett squinted as he realized that they had wandered onto the outdoor deck. He felt drawn to the climbing structure, but he could tell that Jeremiah needed to talk to him, so he leaned his arms on the railing and squinted up at his friend. Jeremiah was obviously relieved that Everett was staying as he followed suit.

"It just bothers me that Kabe and I seemed to be such good friends during our ORIENTATION. I thought that it would stay that way, but now he only wants to be around *Jace*. He knows that Jace bullied me. He even saw it happen. It just hurts my feelings that he spends so much time with someone that was so mean to me," Jeremiah said, scowling as he brushed a crumb off of his vest.

Everett nodded. Objectively he could understand that Kabe was spending time with Jace because they were family, but he could also understand why Jeremiah was upset with Kabe over having a friendship with someone that had bullied him.

They spent a few minutes in companionable silence before Jeremiah sighed and said that he needed to work on an assignment. Everett was about to admit that he needed to do the same when he felt the familiar panic rise in his stomach. He was overwhelmed because he knew that he was behind on his assignments. He had not worked on any of them after Landon Perry's call. His seminar had taught him that he avoided work when he was afraid that it would not be perfect, and now he knew that he needed to work past those feelings.

He left the rec center with the intention of heading to his room to do some work. He decided that if he chose just one small activity to complete, like adding his star data to his chart, he would not feel as overwhelmed as he would if he tried to get everything done.

Everett walked slowly and was mentally prioritizing his assignments as he crossed through the lobby to get to his dorm room. He pulled up short when he saw a large crowd gathered near the lobby's entrance. Curiosity overcame him, and he walked over to the crowd to see what they were looking at.

The Chancellor, Dre, and a crowd of workers were standing at the front of the lobby. The Chancellor was gesturing at the ceiling as a giant poster was being hung in an archway. Several workers were grappling with the corners of the poster, trying to keep them from folding in as they hung the poster. The crowd of students that were watching the procedure clapped and cheered when the poster was finally installed.

The poster was a huge picture of Landon Perry in his astronaut uniform superimposed over an image of a younger Landon Perry wearing the SFGP uniform. Since Everett was avoiding his Landon Perry file, he had not seen a picture of Perry as a boy. He swallowed as he looked at the dark hair on Landon's forehead and the proud gleam in his eyes.

No matter where I travel in this universe, The School for Gifted Potentials will always be my home was written in bold royal blue letters across the bottom of the poster.

The Chancellor nodded with satisfaction to dismiss the workers and then turned to listen to something that Dre was saying. Everett's stomach twisted in knots. His plan to go back to his room to work was forgotten as he decided to escape to his laboratory until his next class started instead.

Everett hurried to the dining hall that evening feeling flustered and uneasy. Kimin had called and demanded that he meet her for dinner, saying that it was urgent. Receiving the call from Landon Perry had derailed his plans to work on his assignments the night before, so he felt anxious about the amount of work that he needed to accomplish that night, but he knew that Kimin must have a good reason for pulling him away from his studies.

He frowned with concern as he grabbed a quick meal and found her already seated with Sonniy and Jeremiah at a table in the back of the room.

Kimin's foot tapped impatiently as she waited for the others to arrive. Not feeling brave enough to chat with Sonniy and Jeremiah because of Kimin's mood, Everett picked at his dinner and scanned the room along with Kimin for their other friends.

Kabe arrived next, although the look on his face told Everett that he had not come willingly. CiCi slipped into the seat next to Everett, and he smiled at her.

"Hey, where did you sneak in from?" he whispered to her playfully.

She flashed a secretive smile and said, "I have a secret entrance."

They giggled, which earned them a scowl from Kimin.

The group ate in awkward silence as they waited for Greta to arrive. After everyone had cleaned their plates, Kimin finally threw up her hands in exasperation.

"Well, I guess Greta isn't coming," she said with a scowl. Everett flushed and felt his stomach drop. He did not like the tone that Kimin was using about his best friend.

"So, why did you need all of us to meet you here?" Sonniy finally asked, sounding a trifle annoyed.

Everyone turned to look at Kimin. She leaned forward and motioned for them to do the same. Kabe frowned, but finally complied.

"Well, I just want to tell you all that the *originals* have been bothering me. I have been noticing this since last week. They step in front of me in the hallway, they get in front of me in line at the terminals, and Dre and another girl have been following me around, mocking me whenever I'm talking to a friend. As soon as I turn around to confront them, they start talking about something else. I've had it!" she exclaimed, her cheeks flushing.

Kabe craned his head to look around for *originals*.

"*Kabe!*" Kimin hissed. "I don't want them to know that I am talking about them!"

Kabe frowned and said, "Look Kimin, some of this sounds like it could be accidental. Maybe they are intentionally cutting you off, but maybe they just aren't paying attention and you're just sensitive to their actions because of your ORIENTATION.

Maybe next time you should just say something to them about it. I can help you if you want."

Kimin's jaw dropped, and she crossed her arms.

"So you think that I am just making this up?" she yelped defensively.

"Kabe, I think that Kimin is saying that this *keeps* happening, so it doesn't feel like they are doing it by accident," CiCi interjected, earning a smile from Kimin.

"Well, like I said, it's possible that they are doing it on purpose, but it's also not obvious stuff, like the stuff that they did during our ORIENTATIONS, so maybe it is just a coincidence is what *I'm* saying," Kabe replied, his face darkening.

"Oh you probably just don't think that the *originals* do anything wrong since your *cousin* is one of them," Kimin said spitefully, not liking that Kabe was not giving her the sympathy that she had expected.

"Kimin, that's not fair," Everett said, shocked by her behavior. "Kabe is just trying to show you the other side of the argument, so that you can see it from another viewpoint. Maybe you should calm down for a moment and consider what he said."

Kimin squeaked at Everett's words and was about to respond when she caught sight of Greta hurrying up to the table.

Greta stopped short when she looked around and saw the tension on her friends' faces.

"What is going on?" she breathed.

"Where *were* you?" Kimin snapped, now irate over the way her problem was being received.

"I, well, I'm sorry, but I had already eaten when you called, and I was in the middle of an assignment. I hurried to get over here…" Greta trailed off, her eyes looking at everyone's faces.

"You know Greta, sometimes people are more important than projects," Kimin retorted.

Greta flushed and then went pale.

"I'm sorry Kimin," she whispered, struggling past tears. "I didn't know it was that important to you. You didn't tell me why you wanted to meet up."

Everett frowned at Kimin, while Kabe stood up and put his arm around Greta's shoulders.

"Look Kimin, it sounds like you are mad at Dre, not at Greta. I think that we should all go back to our rooms and meet up later, once everyone has calmed down a little bit," Kabe said authoritatively.

Everett stood up slowly to show that he agreed with Kabe. CiCi hesitated and then stood up with them. Kimin glared at Sonniy and Jeremiah, and they remained seated.

Kimin sniffed.

"I don't think that I need time to calm down," she said icily. "I think that I just need friends that can make time to listen to me when I'm upset and help me come up with ways to solve my problems."

Everett took a step back in astonishment.

"Are you saying that you don't want to be friends anymore?" he asked, shocked by this sudden turn of events.

Kimin hesitated and then stubbornly crossed her arms. Kabe scowled as a quiet sob escaped from Greta, and he gently led her away. CiCi hesitated for a moment and then scurried to Greta's side. Everett stood for a long moment with his eyes on Kimin. She was flushed, although he was not sure if it was from anger or embarrassment. Finally, he shook his head, glared at Sonniy and Jeremiah, and strode out of the room.

He caught up with Greta, Kabe, and CiCi in the hallway. Greta's shoulders shook with tears that she was trying to hide. Kabe had his hands in his pockets and was staring at a refreshment terminal to make it appear that he did not notice, and CiCi was making soft noises as she kindly stroked Greta's arm.

Everett and Kabe locked eyes for a moment before Kabe cleared his throat.

"Does anyone want to go for a walk? I know how to get to an outdoor track," he offered.

Greta sniffed and nodded, so they all turned to follow Kabe. He led them through the lobby to an elevator that Everett had never noticed before. They all got in, and even Greta shivered a little with anticipation. It was always exciting to discover something novel about their new home. Kabe punched in a code on the keypad, and the elevator shot up. Greta and CiCi clutched each other with nervous anticipation.

The elevator stopped and opened to the roof. The world had fallen into twilight, the most peaceful time of day for Everett. He scanned the area and saw that a track wound around the entire perimeter of the school's roof. Other tracks wound in concentric loops from the center to the edge of the roof to create five tracks of varying lengths.

CiCi let out a joyous laugh and raced to look over the edge of the building. Panicked, Greta called out to her, but Kabe reassured her that there was no way that CiCi could fall. The track was surrounded by an almost invisible netting of incredible strength, so their young friend was in no danger.

Greta nodded, and the trio began to walk around the largest track on the outer perimeter of the roof. CiCi skipped back to them when her curiosity had been sated.

"How did you find out about this place?" Everett asked.

Kabe shrugged.

"Jace showed it to me," he replied, looking almost embarrassed to mention the *original's* name.

Everett glanced over at Greta and saw that she was walking with her arms wrapped around herself, staring at the ground.

"I hope that you know that Kimin was wrong," he finally said to her, startling his friends somewhat. "You don't care more about your projects than your friends. Kimin was cryptic when she called me about why she needed to meet as well. You couldn't have known that it was so important to her."

Kabe nodded.

"I almost didn't go," he admitted with a shrug. "I had a lot to get done tonight too, but she was insistent. It was not okay for her to be rude to you. We agreed that we needed to feel free to make choices for ourselves in this group without the fear of someone getting mad at us."

Everett and Greta looked at each other. They both recalled the conversation that they'd had as a group during their ORIENTATION.

"That's right," Greta whispered, remembering. A tear slipped down her cheek. "I know that Kimin was wrong to say those things to me, but I still want us all to be friends."

Kabe, Everett, and CiCi nodded.

"Let's wait and see what happens tomorrow," CiCi finally said with a hopefulness in her voice that caused Everett and Greta to smile, but caused Kabe to frown with doubt.

Pangs of Remorse

Everett woke up the following day feeling tired and sore. The conflict that he was experiencing about Perry's visit and the argument with Kimin had kept him up most of the night. He could not believe that his group of friends had shattered so easily. He knew that they all had favorites within the group, but it still shocked him that there was so little loyalty as a whole.

As he ordered his breakfast, he thought back on Jeremiah's comment that Kimin was the only one that had kept in touch with him. It did not surprise Everett that Jeremiah was loyal to Kimin, but he had to know that it was wrong for Kimin to be rude to Greta and then declare that she needed better friends, so Everett was surprised that Jeremiah had gone along with her. He was a little surprised by Sonniy as well. Even though Kimin was her best friend, she had also not put up with Kimin's immature behavior in the past, so he wasn't sure why Sonniy had not stood up to Kimin this time.

Maybe we weren't as good of friends as I had believed, Everett thought sadly as he headed out the door to class.

His skin prickled as he walked through the halls on his way to class. Although he rarely saw Kimin, Sonniy, or Jeremiah in the halls because they had such different schedules, he still felt anxious about running into one of them.

What would he do if he said hello and they ignored him?

His emotions were in turmoil throughout the day. During his free time, he hid in his laboratory, catching up on his assignments. He threw himself into the work and surprised himself by completing several good revisions on his experimental design. A rush of adrenaline spiked through him when he received a message from Ms. Everlay praising his work. He knew that she was anxious about his presentation as well, but he was still surprised by her almost instant feedback.

That evening, Everett met up with Greta and CiCi in Greta's room. The trio lay down on their stomachs to work, and they happily swung their legs in the air as they tapped away on their SKEtch pads. They were each working on independent assignments but wanted the security of each other's presence. Although no one had admitted it, they were avoiding eating in the dining hall because they were not sure what they would do if they ran into Kimin, Sonniy, or Jeremiah. They had eaten quickly in their rooms and were using their social time to study together.

They were mostly quiet, but every once in a while Everett would ask for advice on what he was writing, or Greta would shyly ask for his input on the design of her experiment. CiCi was completely absorbed in the story that she was reading.

When Greta noticed Everett push his hair off of his forehead for the third time, she playfully reached out to tug on a long, dark lock.

"If your hair bothers you so much, why don't you just get it cut? My clothes bothered my SENSUAL OVEREXCITABILITY, so Mr. Elan said that the easiest managing strategy was to remove the irritation. Is there a reason why you want to keep your hair long like that?" she asked.

"Are you trying to look like Landon Perry?" CiCi added teasingly.

Everett's heart caught in his throat at her comment.

He swallowed uncomfortably. He had not shared his hunch that Landon might be his father with his friends and did not think that he ever would. His mother had always kept his hair this way, and now he wondered if it had been to remind her of Landon. His stomach twisted, and he rolled onto his back and took a deep breath.

"You're right," he finally said, trying to sound unaffected. "There is no good reason to put up with this irritation. Where can I get it cut?"

Greta sent him a map of the location via her SKEtch pad, and he thanked her casually.

She smiled and turned back to her work, unaware that he had just made an important and difficult decision. Cutting off his hair would be like severing a tie to his mother. After what he had learned about her and what he suspected about her, though, he rebelliously thought that severing that tie was just what he needed.

After he left Greta's room, he followed the map that she had sent him to the personal care section of the SFGP. A humanoid robot greeted him as he entered. He was a far cry from the machinelike Sev that had helped him through his ORIENTATION. This robot had two arms and legs and had a humanlike face with features that moved.

"How may I help you?" it asked in a smooth, authoritative voice.

"I need a haircut," Everett said, swallowing hard.

"Right this way," the robot replied and gestured toward a tall, thin stool.

As soon as Everett sat down, the robot covered his uniform with a silky, lightweight cloth and pulled out a variety of tools.

"What kind of haircut would you like?" the robot asked.

"Well, I guess I need to have a haircut that keeps my hair off of my forehead," Everett said unsurely.

The robot nodded with understanding.

"That is a frequent request for those with the SENSUAL OVEREXCITABILITY," the robot replied.

Before Everett could respond, the robot cut off his long bangs with a few deft strokes.

As he looked at himself in the mirror, Everett was surprised to find that tears were coursing down his cheeks. He reached up out of habit to smooth the hair off of his forehead and sobbed when he encountered bare skin.

He had not realized how attached he was to his hair until it was gone. His mother had always loved his hair. Countless nights had been spent with him lying on her stomach to read. She had always read with her book in one hand as the other hand toyed with his long bangs.

Whenever he was upset, she would reach out to lift the hair off his forehead, and he had done the same for her the few times that he had seen her upset. The tender gesture of lifting his hair had been a symbol of their affection for each other, and he sobbed uncontrollably at the loss.

It was too much freedom, too final for him to bear.

He had thought that he was ready to sever the tie with his mother, but he had been wrong.

He had gone through his ORIENTATION and his first weeks of classes with the vague idea that his mother would come back for him at some point. It was possible that she had wanted to give him a taste of the school so that he could choose what he wanted, and he had been waiting for her to come back, to ask him if he wanted to come home.

But she had not come back, and for the first time, as he stared at his new image, he realized that it was quite possible that she never would.

He returned to his room and went straight to his mirror. His forehead felt tingly, and there was a phantom sensation of hair on it that he could not quite shake. His short, trim hair made him look older and different. A feeling of independence surged through him, and he grabbed his SKEtch pad to start a video call with CiCi.

She squealed when she saw him, the reaction that he had secretly hoped for, and reassured him repeatedly that his hair looked great. He smiled and thanked her, grateful for the reassurance.

Her approval gave him the confidence to call Greta next.

She flushed when she saw him on the screen, and her eyes narrowed as she looked him over.

"Nice haircut Everett. I'd like to come over, is that okay?" she asked, a strange determination in her voice.

He paused, wondering why she wanted to come over. He knew that she had missed a lot of work the previous evening, and they had just studied together.

Realizing that he had paused for too long, he covered his strange behavior with a smile and encouraged her to join him whenever she got the chance.

There was a knock at his door in a matter of minutes. He let her in, and they stood awkwardly by his table for a moment. Shyly, he invited her to sit in his chair, while he leaned on the edge of his desk. She scanned the room and pointed out his ICOTTS poster.

"Yeah, I got that from my advisor," he said with a shrug. "She remembered that I really liked it. I asked her about personalizing our rooms, so she sent me some posters to help me out."

Greta nodded, but her gaze remained on his poster, as if she was uncomfortable making eye contact with him. Trying to think of something that could break the silence, a picture of Kabe's room popped into his mind.

"Kabe added a workout station to his room," he shared. "He sketched it out with Mr. Elan when we learned about the PSYCHOMOTOR OE. He has a bunch of metal bars sticking out of his wall that he can exercise on."

"Yes, I've seen it," she said, finally looking up at him.

"Oh," he replied as the same jealous feeling that he always got where Kabe was concerned crept back. It hurt a little that she had gone to Kabe's room before going to his.

"He asked me to go look at it," she told him apologetically. "I didn't really want to, because I had so much work to do, but I felt that it would be rude to say no."

He shrugged and pushed off of the table to walk around.

"That's nice," he said, trying to sound as if it did not bother him.

She flushed and looked down at her hands. He instantly felt bad about making her uncomfortable, especially since she had come over to see him.

"Sorry Greta," he said sheepishly. "I just get jealous sometimes that you have other friends. I know it's silly, because we both have other friends, so I'm sorry if I made you feel like you had to defend yourself to me."

They shared a smile, and he knew that she understood.

"That's okay, Everett. I feel that way about you spending time with your other friends too," she admitted softly.

They both looked at the poster, not sure how to follow up their admission of jealousy about each other.

"I wonder if I could personalize my space," Greta finally said, breaking the awkward silence.

"I guess you could think about what makes you the happiest and then see if they could put that in your room," he suggested.

Their eyes connected with excitement.

"Plants!" they shouted in unison. Greta grabbed his wrists with enthusiasm.

"We could have them install potted plants all around our rooms!" she exclaimed. She turned to look at the layout of his room. "I would want mine there, over my bed."

She pointed to the large wall behind his bed and noticed the poster of Landon Perry for the first time.

"Oh, that is really nice," she said.

"Thanks," he replied nonchalantly, as if the poster meant the same to him as the ICOTTS poster. "You're right, that would be the best place to put some plants."

He stood on his bed and casually took the poster down, swallowing as he rolled it in his hands.

Trying to sound excited, he turned to her and said, "Let's sketch out some ideas and send them to Ms. Everlay. She would probably know how to get us the materials that we need, and she can help us figure out if our idea will work."

He placed the rolled up poster beside his bed as if it held no meaning for him and grabbed his SKEtch pad. He sat cross-legged on his bed and invited Greta to sit next to him. She curled up next to him and leaned over his shoulder as he sketched out a possible plant setup. She already knew the names of some plants that grew well in small containers, and they added the plant names to their list of materials.

When they were finished, they had created an intricate pattern of small potted plants. They reasoned that they could add a magnetic layer to the wall behind the bed and put the plants in magnetic pots. They spent nearly an hour discussing planting soils, watering systems, and maintenance issues.

"It will be so lovely to go to bed each night surrounded by the smell of plants," Greta said softly after he had sent their idea to their instructor. "I hope that Ms. Everlay can help us make it possible."

He nodded and smiled, full of joy that he had found a friend that understood him so well.

"So, I came over because you seemed upset when CiCi teased you about looking like Landon Perry," Greta said finally, struggling to look him in the eye. "It seems like something about him really bothers you."

She looked meaningfully at the rolled up poster that had been so prominently displayed before her visit. He stopped for a moment, his heart thudding. How could he explain his idea that Landon Perry might be his father when he had never even told Greta how he had ended up at The School for Gifted Potentials? She did not know that his mother had raised him to believe that she was a different person with no connection to the SFGP, or that her brother was the Chancellor, or that she had signed away her rights to him after promising him that they could be together forever.

Greta was a great friend and a wonderful listener, but he was not ready for anyone to know his secrets. She was suspicious of his strange behavior though, so he knew that he had to give her some reason for his odd reaction to hearing about Perry's visit.

"Well, I didn't want anyone to know this, because I don't want it to seem like I am bragging," he started hesitantly. She sat up on her knees and nodded encouragingly. "Landon Perry has requested to see my plant experiment, since I found plants that grow in conditions similar to Mars. He will be coming by my lab to meet me during his visit to our school."

"Is that why you act like you don't want to talk about him? Because you're nervous about meeting him?" she asked quietly with an edge of distrust in her voice.

He swallowed. He could tell her the rest, but this was his only chance to do it.

"Yeah, that's why," he lied, not meeting her eyes. "Don't tell anyone else, okay? I really don't want any extra attention."

Greta hesitated until she realized that if their roles were reversed, she would not want anyone to make a fuss over her, so she nodded. Despite the fact that his explanation made sense, she still felt that he was keeping something from her.

"Well, I'm glad that we worked out a plan to put plants in our rooms," she said abruptly and stood up. "Thanks for having me over, and I know that you will do great when you meet Perry."

She waved farewell and left quickly. Everett knew that she was not fully satisfied with his explanation and probably suspected that he was hiding something. He pushed his face into his hands and pulled his body into a tight ball. He hated deceiving his best friend but could not imagine where or how to start his story.

He pulled in a deep breath, held it, and then forced it out. Pushing himself off of the bed, he vowed that he would not brood the entire night and called CiCi. She was breathless as she answered his video call and said that she was heading out for a late snack in the dining hall with Kabe. She invited him to join them, and he asked her if she would mind calling Greta to invite her as well. After her abrupt exit, he did not feel confident enough to do it himself.

She frowned as if she wondered why he did not just call Greta to invite her himself but readily agreed. Flooded with nervous energy after his talk with Greta, he jogged out of his room to find his friends. They were already in the dining hall, talking and laughing as they waited for a food terminal. The room was bustling despite the late hour, and every conversation seemed to be about the astronaut's arrival the next day.

They grabbed their snacks and looked around for a table. Everett's stomach dropped when he saw Kimin, Sonniy, and Jeremiah huddled together at the edge of a table. He swallowed, knowing that this would be the best time to smooth things over with Kimin. He was about to move over to the small group when Kimin looked up and saw him. She raised her chin haughtily and said something to Sonniy and Jeremiah. The trio quickly gathered their things and strode out of the dining hall together without a backward glance at Everett and his friends.

"Well, I guess that shoots down the theory that everything will be better today," Kabe said with a mirthless smile.

He turned to chat with a tall girl at the table next to them about the events that would be happening the next day. When she got up to leave, he turned back to his friends and leaned in to share the information that he had gathered.

"So, Landon Perry is going to arrive tomorrow morning in a *car*," Kabe shared excitedly. "The Chancellor has given permission for students to watch him arrive, but he didn't make a big announcement, so not everybody knows about it. I say we all go. I want to see his vehicle!"

At that moment, Caspan and Anton spied Everett's small group in the crowd and moved over to their table. Kabe quickly shared the news with them and discovered that the older boys knew even more information about the astronaut's arrival.

"You have to be there early, around dawn," Anton shared conspiratorially. "We could go to the top of the climbing structure and scope out a good spot. I want to be able to see everything."

Kabe nodded eagerly, but Greta shook her head uncomfortably and CiCi made a face.

"Why don't you two go up and take a picture on your SKEtch pads," Caspan suggested. "You can send a picture to our SKEtch pads and then we can all pick a spot to meet."

Kabe looked concerned.

"I don't see how I can climb the monolith if I am holding my SKEtch pad in one hand the whole way," he objected.

Anton grabbed his SKEtch pad by the bottom corner and snapped his wrist. To everyone's amazement, the rigid SKEtch pad rolled up like a piece of paper, creating a tube that was easy to carry. Even Caspan was surprised by this feature.

Anton shrugged and said, "I took a technology INTENSIVE one time. They taught us lots of tricks that the SKEtch pad can do that the instructors never think about showing us."

Everett made a mental note to add that INTENSIVE to the list of classes that he wanted to sign up for.

Kabe snapped his SKEtch pad into a cylinder and put it in his back pocket with a grin. He and Anton hurried out of the room to climb, while everyone else relaxed and talked. Everett felt Greta watching him with concern, so he did his best to appear cheerful and participate in the conversation about the upcoming event. Despite his strange feelings about Perry, Everett couldn't help but get swept up in his friends' excitement. He realized that if his letter to test at the SFGP had come a month later, he would have totally missed the astronaut's visit.

CiCi squealed with excitement when her SKEtch pad vibrated, and everyone grabbed their pads to pull up the photos sent by Anton and Kabe. Everett was impressed by their speed. The group quickly began discussing the best place to meet the following day for the arrival of Perry's car. Even Everett got caught up in the debate, suddenly feeling the need to have the very best spot available.

Kabe and Anton rejoined them, both a little breathless, and pointed out a tree that had seemed like the best location from their vantage point. The others deferred to their judgment, and the group stood up as they realized that they would need to hurry to bed in order to wake up at dawn. Caspan promised to relay the information to Tobias, who was studying in his room, and they left one another with the assurance that they would meet at the tree the following morning.

Despite the weariness of his body, Everett's IMAGINATIONAL OE kept him awake for several hours as he imagined many possible scenarios for the next day. His mind created scenarios ranging from Landon Perry never really arriving, to Landon arriving and embracing Everett as his son. Sheer exhaustion swept him into a light and troubled sleep.

Anticipation and Doubt

Everett emerged from his room tingling with nervous anticipation. He had checked his uniform several times for stray lint and had adjusted the lapels of his crisp white shirt more than a few times. He nervously smoothed his pants with his palms as he moved down the hallway and converged with a small crowd of students headed to watch Landon Perry's arrival.

He hurried through the crowd to a tall aspen tree that was at the top of a small knoll on the west side of the school lawn. He could see that a large crowd was already forming. Not all of the students at the SFGP would be interested in watching the astronaut arrive, but Everett was curious despite his nerves to see how many students were really at the school. He noticed Greta waving excitedly and sped up to meet her.

Despite his mixed feelings about the astronaut, Everett suddenly felt a growing impatience for his arrival. The crowd was increasing and excited murmurs reverberated in the early morning stillness. Everett nervously adjusted his noise reduction implements to tune out the background noises. It felt great to be part of a crowd that shared the same enthusiastic anticipation, but the cacophony of expectant voices caused his nervous stomach to churn.

Slowly, his friends appeared in pairs. Anton and Caspan arrived together, with Kabe and CiCi following close behind. Everett swallowed with disappointment as he thought of the friends that would not be joining him. In that moment, he realized how much he missed them.

"Where is Tobias?" he asked Caspan.

The boy's dark eyes slid over to Everett.

"He said that he would make it if he could," Caspan replied with a shrug. "He had a few things that he wanted to take care of this morning."

Everett nodded and swallowed to hide his disappointment. Somehow, having his friends around him helped him feel more secure about the astronaut's arrival, and he wished that Tobias had joined them.

The sound of cheering drew his attention to the road. The first vehicle of the caravan could now be seen in the distance.

"Some kids are probably here just to see the vehicles," Greta told CiCi in a hushed voice. CiCi grinned and joined hands with Greta.

The other children nodded in agreement. They had all grown up in cities, with the exception of Greta, and had used the POD rail system to travel in. Vehicles operated by people were rare, and they were all excited to see one in person.

As the vehicles drew closer, Everett and his friends began to count them aloud.

"One, two… four… six… seven," they breathed in unison, although they did not realize that they were counting as a group. The sheer number of motorized vehicles in the caravan spoke to the importance of the school's guest speaker. Everett swallowed hard as his stomach dropped.

The vehicles were slim, light, and shaped like torpedoes. They glistened with solar panels and seemed to glide over the earth in an elegant swarm. When they stopped, just past the last group of students, a collective hush fell over the crowd as they waited to see the passengers get out. There was a long pause, and Everett craned his neck to see why the cars had not opened yet.

Finally, he spotted the Chancellor, who had just arrived at the front of the first car. His arms were open wide and an uncustomary smile covered his face. The door of the first vehicle opened, and the crowd exploded with cheers as Landon Perry's tall figure emerged from it. He embraced the Chancellor for a moment and then turned to wave at the crowd. The cheers grew louder and louder, until the Chancellor put his arm around the astronaut's shoulders and led him toward the village of tents that had been constructed for his visit.

The cheers died down to murmurs and laughter. Most of the students started to head back to the school and their morning classes, while some stayed to watch as the other members of Perry's group got out of their vehicles. Everett noticed with interest that many of them pulled out bags and unusual looking equipment.

"That was exciting, but I need to get to class," Anton finally said.

Everett reluctantly pulled his attention away from the cars and saw that most of his friends looked anxious to leave now that the event was over. It distressed him for a moment. He knew that he should go to class as well, but something kept him from moving, so he nodded curtly and forced a smile to show his friends that they could leave.

Caspan stepped forward to pat him on the shoulder. He could sense that Everett needed support, although he could never have fathomed why. The others followed suit as they turned to leave. CiCi threw him a final, concerned look over her shoulder as she fell into step with Kabe.

It took him a moment, but he realized that Greta had stayed. He looked at her in surprise, knowing that it must have been difficult for her to wait for him. She was no doubt worried about missing time in class. He squeezed her shoulder and smiled to show her that he was touched.

"Thanks for hanging out with me Greta. I think that I might stay a while, but you can go ahead and get to class," he told her, trying to conceal the catch in his voice.

She searched his face, but he avoided meeting her eyes.

"Why do you need to stay?" she asked with a stubborn determination in her voice. "You were so excited about Landon Perry during our ORIENTATION. Learning about him is your long-term goal. You said that you are nervous about presenting

~ 97 ~

your experiment to him, but it seems like there is something else about him that bothers you."

Everett nodded. Suddenly he wanted more than anything to share his story with Greta, to unburden himself of the story of his mother's trick, his discovery about her past, and his questions about Landon Perry. Just as he opened his mouth to tell her, a campus monitor came forward and informed them that the Chancellor had instructed him to hurry any students that remained back to class.

Greta sighed. She felt as though her friend had been about to open up to her. They parted ways with a promise to get together for a midday meal.

It was a long and confusing day for Everett. When he got back to his room that evening, he realized that he could not remember anything that had happened that day with any clarity. It felt like he had been going through the motions of talking and eating, but the only thing that he could recall with absolute distinction was the moment that Landon Perry had stepped out of his vehicle.

At that moment, Everett had thought, *that is my father*.

Chills coursed through him as he considered that thought. If Landon Perry really was his father, he had to wonder why the man had never contacted him. If Landon Perry was not his father, he still had a major piece of information about himself that he was missing and might never know.

As Everett turned on his SKEtch pad to call Greta, hoping to distract himself from his thoughts, he noticed the *accept* button flashing on the wall. A sense of dread washed over him, filling his veins with fire, as he knew that it must be from Perry. He pushed the *accept* button without realizing that he had lifted his arm.

"Good evening Everett. I reviewed the changes that you made to your experimental design. I sent you a few minor corrections to make, but I am also contacting you to give you a new assignment. At several points in your experiment, you made changes to your experimental conditions, such as light and soil adjustments. I want you to write a paper that defends your reasons for making those changes. You can pretend that a scientific panel has called your design into question, or you can pretend that the INTELLEX crew is your audience. I look forward to seeing your first draft by tomorrow."

Everett heaved a sigh of relief as his technical writing instructor completed her message. He was relieved that it had not been the message that he had feared. It also gave him something new to focus on, a distraction that he desperately needed. He dove into the assignment with relief.

Not wanting to think about the INTELLEX crew in any way, he used his IMAGINATIONAL OE to create an imaginary panel of scientific experts and pictured himself standing in front of them. He imagined that the entire wall behind him was a surface wall, like the wall in Ms. Everlay's office, and that it had a picture of his lab room projected alongside his data.

As he wrote, he imagined using the surface wall to create a timeline of events and added the changes that he had made and why he made them to the timeline as he spoke passionately to the panel. When he was done, he reread his work with surprise. It was actually a great first draft.

An unexpected yawn indicated that he had stayed up later than usual, and he crawled into bed thinking happily about his paper, with thoughts of Landon Perry pushed deep into the back of his mind.

Everett awoke the next morning with the strange sensation that he did not know where he was. He had slept deeply, and for a moment, he felt as though he was waking up in his mother's apartment.

Was The School for Gifted Potentials just a dream?

He kept his eyes squeezed shut, hoping to keep the feeling that he might wake up to see his mother for as long as possible. After a while, he opened his eyes with a sigh. He knew in his heart that it had not been a dream. His mother truly had abandoned him, and he needed to start accepting it.

He dressed quickly and was heading to order his breakfast when he saw that a video message was waiting for him. He watched the *accept* button blink, over and over, for a long moment. This time he knew with certainty that the call would be from Landon Perry.

After a moment of hesitation, he turned away from the button and ordered his meal. Something told him that this would feel like the longest day of his life.

When his tray arrived, he sat down and ate his food slowly, prolonging each bite, hoping to put off the inevitable message. Eventually there was nothing left on his plate, so he methodically cleaned up his tray and straightened his clothing before venturing over to the button to press *accept*.

"Good morning Everett. Dr. Perry has requested to see your lab experiment today. You have been excused from your morning classes so that you can present it to him. Due to his complex schedule, he could not give an exact time of arrival, but please be in your lab by seven in the morning. I will join you and we can work on your experiment until he arrives. If there is still time left after his visit, you can return to your classes or take advantage of some additional time in the rec center before the assembly starts. I'll see you soon!"

Ms. Everlay's face disappeared from the screen, and Everett heaved a sigh of relief. Although the message had been about seeing Perry, the fact that the information had been delivered by his instructor made it easier to deal with.

He moved to his mirror and mechanically adjusted his uniform. He ran his fingers through his cropped hair and adjusted his vest. After a sigh of resignation, he walked out of his room and headed slowly to his lab. He imagined that he would sit in the room for hours and would only see the astronaut and his entourage for a brief moment before he left to continue his tour of the school.

As he entered his lab, he was overwhelmed to find that it was filled with people. Perplexed by this invasion of his space, he searched for Ms. Everlay in the dim light.

She smiled when she saw him and pushed her way to the door to grab his arm.

"Attention, please. I would like to take the opportunity to introduce Everett. This experiment was designed by him, and I would like to give him a few moments to explain his experiment to you," she said to the group and then smiled encouragingly at him.

He felt trapped as he looked around at the strangers in the room. Their G tattoos were evident despite the dim lighting, and the sheer number of people startled him. All he could think about was the safety of his experiment. It was not a large room, and he kept picturing that someone's stray elbow or SKEtch pad would disturb one of his plants.

Everett turned his back to the group for a moment as he struggled through his anxiety. As he breathed slowly, he recalled the technical writing paper in which he had described his experimental setup and the reasoning behind it to a pretend panel of experts, and he knew that he already had the information that he needed for the impromptu presentation.

His cheeks cooled and his confidence mounted as he turned around to face his audience. He did not actually look at them and focused on an image of Sonniy in his mind's eye, since she had been his audience in his first paper.

An hour passed swiftly as he described his scientific query, the plants and growing conditions that he had selected, and the data that he had gathered to that point. It helped that he had the complete attention of his audience. After a while, he stopped thinking of Sonniy as his audience and began to connect with the people in the room.

When he finished talking, a stillness hung in the air for a long moment, and he realized that he had captivated his audience. The dim light concealed the flush of pride that warmed his face. A murmur began in the back of the room, and soon the entire room was buzzing. From what he could hear, they were having a true discourse about his work. They did not give only praise because he was a child. He could tell that they were evaluating his work on a scientific level, and it filled him with pride and awe that they respected his work enough to judge it critically.

Just as he was beginning to feel comfortable enough to circulate among them, a sudden hush silenced the conversations in the room. Everyone was staring at the doorway. Everett felt his stomach drop, and he slowly turned around. Landon Perry's tall frame filled the doorway, and after taking in the scene for a moment, he walked in. He was tall and handsome. The dim light somehow illuminated the man's dark, glittering eyes, and his G tattoo stood out at the base of his neck.

Everett noticed that a crowd of people stood behind the astronaut and were peering into the room over his shoulder, but the room was already filled to capacity.

Landon seemed to notice the same thing.

"Good morning. It encourages me to see that the faculty at The School for Gifted Potentials continues to support and encourage the efforts of its students. Unfortunately, laboratories never seem to be large enough. I hope that you won't mind if I meet briefly with this student and his instructor alone," Landon said in a clear, commanding voice.

The crowd seemed to be in momentary awe of him and did not immediately process his meaning. Suddenly, in a flurry of activity, the people in the room excused themselves one by one, most stopping briefly to greet the astronaut on their way out. As the last person left, Landon closed the door behind them. Everett caught the Chancellor's surprised cough as the door closed, leaving him in the hallway with the rest of Perry's entourage.

Landon took a long, deep breath and held it in for a moment before he pushed the air out of his lungs. Everett realized that it must be overwhelming to the man to be constantly surrounded by people eager to gain his attention. He flushed with pride as he noticed that Landon was moving slowly through the room, looking at the experimental setups and the data feed with interest. Finally, he turned to look at Everett in the dim light.

"So, we finally meet," he said softly, smiling to set the boy at ease. "I am happy to meet you, since we obviously share some of the same passionate interest in finding plants that can grow on Mars. Your instructor sent your technical writing piece to me. I am impressed by your experimental design and the thinking behind it, and with the thoughtful adjustments that you made along the way. I find your work quite intriguing and very disciplined. Your file indicates that you were only at this school for a week when you set up this experiment. I am curious to know how you have developed such strong, scientific reasoning skills without the benefit of being at this school."

Although the light was dim, Everett saw a genuine curiosity in the man's eyes.

"My mother raised me to think like a scientist," he replied, trying to modulate his voice to sound normal. "She and I used to set up science experiments at home."

Landon's eyes softened.

"It sounds like you had a wonderful mother. You are lucky that she was able to tap into your passion. I am intrigued by your use of a prehistoric plant and a modern plant that are both used to growing in extreme cold and with limited light. The Chancellor has graciously requested a few of the seeds for me to take on my next trip to Mars. I would like to be in touch with you once I have them planted there. Would that be acceptable to you?" Landon asked.

For a moment, Everett felt like he had floated away from his body and was looking down at himself.

He wants to stay in contact with me, as if I am a valued colleague?

"Of course," he finally stuttered. "If there are any further developments in my research, I will let you know about them as well."

The astronaut nodded and sighed as he looked around the lab one last time. Everett could see that the scientist in him would have loved to spend hours in the quiet room, but his schedule would not permit it. The astronaut shook Everett's hand as he thanked him and his instructor for their time and diligent work, and then he was gone.

Everett sank to the floor, feeling like he had just climbed the monolith. His teacher thought that he was blown away by the important man's visit and told him to take as long as he needed to collect himself before he headed back to class.

He sat in the dimly lit room for several hours after his instructor left him.

All that he could think was, *I think that I just met my father.*

Change of Heart

When Everett finally shook himself out of his pensive thoughts and went to find a meal, someone jostled him in the hallway and he nearly fell down. His head whipped to the side to see who had bumped into him, and he was surprised to see Diedre's angry face.

"Did you have a nice visit with our special guest?" she sneered. "He can't talk about anything but *the boy with the plant experiment.*"

Her arms were crossed over her chest, and she leaned forward to use her larger size to intimidate him. As he looked into her eyes, he saw jealousy and spite, and his fear of her vanished.

"I guess it bothers you that a *transplant* has captured the attention of Landon Perry, while he has probably barely registered your existence, despite the Chancellor parading you around in front of him since he got here," Everett spat back.

Diedre paled and then grew red at his words. No *transplant* had ever talked to her that way before. He had also hit on exactly what was making her feel like lashing out at him.

She stalked away from him with her hands clenched in tight fists. Everett could tell that showing her that she did not intimidate him had won the battle, but had probably just started a war. He shrugged. She had clashed with him more than once in his few short weeks at this school, and he knew that this would not be their last confrontation.

Landon Perry can't stop talking about me?

"Everett! Everett!" CiCi cried from the dining hall.

She was standing on a seat, waving frantically at him over the crowd. A huge grin cracked his face, and he hurriedly grabbed his meal before he made his way to the table.

"You didn't tell us that Landon Perry was going to meet you!" she squealed as soon as he sat down. "Everyone is talking about it! You are the only student that he made an appointment to see. Why didn't you tell us?"

Everett flushed and briefly met Greta's eyes. He had shared the secret with her, and he was grateful that she had kept her promise.

"I didn't want to make a big deal about it," he replied with a shrug and took a huge bite of his roasted squash.

"What was he like?" Greta asked shyly, and they all leaned forward to hear his response. Even Kabe could not keep an excited grin from his face as he waited for Everett's answer.

"Well, he is really tall. He was really interested in how I set up my experiment and... he wants to repeat my experiment on Mars," he told them shyly.

CiCi squealed with excitement, while Kabe, Greta, and Caspan looked impressed.

"So you met your hero and have already earned his respect. That's pretty impressive," Kabe told him with a grin.

For once, Everett did not bristle at Kabe and just took the compliment for what it was.

A commotion began as the lights dimmed and then grew brighter. There was a flurry of activity as students cleared their tables and began to push their way out of the dining hall.

"It's time for the assembly!" Anton shouted, pushing through the crowd to find his friends. Caspan jumped up and the others quickly followed suit. They joined hands to stay together as they merged into the swarm of students heading outside to the assembly.

The field in front of the tents had been transformed. A large stage dominated the field, surrounded by thousands and thousands of chairs. By the time that Everett and his friends arrived, most of the chairs were filled with eager students. His group quickly agreed to move to the back and off to the side so that they could find enough seats to sit together. Everett saw Tobias making his way over to them and grabbed an extra chair.

The others greeted him elatedly as they sat down, leaning over one another to discuss what they could see while they waited for the thrilling event to begin. Greta sat next to Everett and gently squeezed his arm.

"Are you okay?" she asked sincerely. "It felt like you wanted to tell me something yesterday morning, but we were interrupted."

He recalled the moment on the hill, when he had been about to tell Greta the story of his mother's lies and about the possibility that Perry was his father. A deep sense of relief overcame him as he realized that he had been spared from a conversation that he was not ready to have yet.

He shook his head and tried to smile convincingly.

"I'm okay. I was just worried about how my experiment would be perceived," he told her, unable to meet her eyes as he lied.

She was quiet for a moment, and he felt that she wanted to press him for more information, but she just squeezed his arm again and turned to listen to Kabe, who was pointing out a raised circle that protruded from the ground. He said that holographic images of the presenters would project throughout the crowd on a multitude of such circles.

"It will be so realistic that it will seem like the person speaking is actually right in front of us," he told her.

Everett turned as he felt a tap on his shoulder. He was surprised to see Kimin, Sonniy, and Jeremiah standing next to him.

Kimin crossed her arms and pushed out her hip.

"Look, I know that Landon Perry is really important to you Everett, so I wanted to be here with you for his presentation. If you don't want us here though, we can leave," she said, sounding defensive and a little scared.

He softened. It was never easy for Kimin to admit that she was wrong and this came pretty close to an apology. At the very least, it showed that she still cared about him.

"Thanks Kimin. I'd love to sit with you all for the presentation," he said, smiling tentatively at Sonniy and Jeremiah.

He stood up to let them pass by him to reach the chairs at the end of the row. As Kimin passed Greta, she spontaneously reached out and embraced her in an apologetic hug. Sonniy squeezed Everett's arm as she shuffled past him, and Jeremiah patted his shoulder. Everett felt a glimmer of hope that the tension would soon be behind them as his friends settled into their seats.

The crowd hushed quickly when the image of the Chancellor suddenly appeared in the circle in front of them. Everett was fascinated by the projection. It did in fact look as though he would contact a real person if he reached out to touch the hologram.

"Good afternoon faculty, students, and honored guests," the Chancellor began, his strong voice reverberating throughout the field. "We have gathered today to honor the accomplishments of a dear friend of mine, Landon Perry of the INTELLEX crew."

The Chancellor paused with a permissive smile as the field erupted with cheers from the students.

"Landon enrolled at The School for Gifted Potentials as a young student with SPECIFIC ACADEMIC APTITUDES in math and reading, but quickly made an impact with the faculty and his peers with his STRENGTH in LEADERSHIP and his passion for science. He utilized his LEADERSHIP qualities and his CREATIVE THINKING ABILITY to envision a wing that could house all of the equipment and faculty needed for MASTERY students working in the field of life science to have a home at The School for Gifted Potentials, now called the Life and Natural Sciences Wing."

A cheer from the center of the field erupted, which Everett assumed must be where the science MASTERY students were seated, and the Chancellor chuckled at their enthusiasm.

"Once Landon completed his MASTERY studies and received the honored G tattoo, he decided to further his education and joined an elite astronaut training program. He took his passion for life science with him all the way to the planet Mars, where he has been researching the possibility of creating life on the lifeless planet."

Cheers interrupted the Chancellor again, but this time they came from around the field. Thousands of voices united to show their respect for the astronaut and his accomplishments.

After giving the students some time to cheer, the Chancellor finally held up one hand to silence the crowd.

"Please allow me to introduce Landon Perry."

The Chancellor bowed his head in respect and backed away. The circle was momentarily empty but was soon filled with the strong, impressive image of Landon. The crowd roared with enthusiasm, and then the entire field fell silent as they waited to hear what the astronaut had to say.

"Thank you, valued Gifted Potentials, for taking time away from your studies to greet me with such kindness and enthusiasm. Being back at this school has been a bittersweet and wonderful journey for me. I realize that while so much at this school has changed since I left, so much of it has also stayed the same. I must take a moment to thank the faculty. When I left my home and became a full-time student at The School for Gifted Potentials, many of the instructors that welcomed me and helped me learn about and develop my STRENGTHS are still here today. In particular, I would like to thank Mr. Dodd. You were a new teacher when I started my ORIENTATION, but you helped me understand myself in a way that has helped me so many times throughout my life, both in school and later, in my career as an astronaut. Thank you for helping me understand my POTENTIAL."

Landon was forced to stop speaking by the ferocious roar of applause that erupted from the student body. Tears were evident on many faces, because most of the students shared Landon's view of the wonderful Mr. Dodd. Everett wiped his own tears away as he realized that the same man who had helped him through his own difficult first week at the school had also helped his father, and maybe even his mother.

Landon let the applause die down naturally, allowing Mr. Dodd to get the accolades that he richly deserved.

"I would also like to thank Ms. Rosenthal. My friends and I had the idea and the passion needed for the development of the Life and Natural Sciences Wing, but you helped us make our dream become a reality. It seems that I have been given all of the glory for the creation of that wing today, but I did not work, or dream, alone. That leads me to what I want to talk to you about today," he said, clearing his throat.

He pulled a stool to the center of the stage and sat down. The audience leaned forward to hear what he would say next, and Everett felt an incredible sense of déjà vu as he recalled his dream about the astronaut's speech.

"I have considered what I would like to talk about today for many months, ever since I received the invitation to come back to The School for Gifted Potentials. At first, I thought for sure that you would want to hear my stories about the astronaut training program, or about traveling to Mars. Then I thought that maybe I would go back to my days as a student and talk about the creation of the Life and Natural Sciences Wing. As I considered what I could talk about, though, I realized that I should think about what *I* would have wanted to hear about when I was a student here. I would not want to hear about something that I could find out on my own. Granted, telling you about Mars would be exciting, but you could also pick up a book about my journeys there or watch a documentary about it. I even wrote an autobiography if you ever want to hear my own take on the events. No, the more I thought about it, the more I realized that I would want to hear about something more personal. I am here today to share pieces of myself with you, because I hope that it will help some of you as you go through your journey as a Gifted Potential."

He cleared his throat again and shifted on his stool. Everett could hear it creak because the audience was absolutely silent.

"I began my career as a student at The School for Gifted Potentials when I was eight years old. My parents were both G, but I had managed to completely exhaust them with my endless questions and yearning to know more, and they thought that I would find the stimulation that I craved as a student at this school. During my ORIENTATION, I discovered that I had the INTELLECTUAL, IMAGINATIONAL, and EMOTIONAL OEs. I was enrolled as a full-time student, and I have to admit that the first few months were difficult. Fortunately, I found some very special friends that became a second family to me. I suspect that many of you are sitting with friends that you met in your ORIENTATION right now, as well as with friends that you connected with in your later studies."

Everett and his friends shared smiles with one another as Landon's words touched them. A tear slipped down Kimin's face, and she reached over to squeeze Greta's shoulder.

"As I grew up here, and I studied, and I developed myself as a leader, a learner, and an innovator, I always looked *forward*. I thought about earning the G tattoo, a lot. I thought about my future career. I will admit, I also dreamt about the possibility of fame. In all of that forward thinking, though, I forgot about the importance of the relationships that helped me achieve my goals, and my dreams. I forgot to thank my instructors, for their tireless work and dedication to me, their student. I forgot to think about my parents and the sacrifice that they made to send me here.

They lost a son so that he could gain a future. Most of all, though, I forgot to thank my friends. The friends that listened to me talk for hours about my problems, about my plans, and about my dreams. The friends that put aside their work on days that I needed someone to spend time with. The friends that brought me gently back to reality when I needed it and pushed me beyond my limits when I needed that."

Perry's voice caught, and he paused for a long moment, pinching the bridge of his nose as if he was too emotional to continue.

"That is my message to you today," he continued finally. "The future will come, and you will be ready for it, or you won't be. Either way, this school will have prepared you for it. Trust in that. So take the time to be a friend, to help a friend, and to enjoy your friends. Most of all, throughout the years, don't forget to *thank* your friends."

He paused for a long, long moment, seeming to be lost in reflection. A few of the younger students began to rustle, which snapped him out of his thoughts.

"Thank you, Gifted Potentials. I have been blessed to see some of your work in my time here at The School for Gifted Potentials, and I know that our world is a better place because of *your* ideas and dreams. Again, I thank you for giving up your precious time to sit with me today."

A smattering of applause began, and he smiled, causing the field to erupt one last time in a commotion of clapping hands and shouting voices. Many of the students stood up or turned to talk with their friends. CiCi, Sonniy, and Kimin started to chatter about his speech immediately.

Everett could not take his eyes off of the hologram. His father sat on the stool for a long moment with his eyes in a faraway place, and Everett wondered if he might be thinking of Camilla. The Chancellor clapped him on the back, and the astronaut stood up to shake hands with the many people that were gathered in places of honor on the stage.

Everett watched it all, wishing that he knew for sure that the man on the stage belonged to him.

My mother must have loved him so much. What could have happened between them?

Greta looked from Everett's face, to the hologram, and back. Suddenly, a chill coursed down her back as she guessed his secret. They had joked with Everett about looking like the astronaut, but seeing her friend's expression confirmed what she would never ask him. Impulsively, she threw her arms around his shoulders, knowing that he needed her support. Her gesture startled him, but thinking about Landon's message, he leaned into her embrace, grateful that he had a friend that understood him.

After talking and laughing in their seats for nearly an hour, the student body slowly began to trickle back into the building. The stage had cleared directly after the speech had ended. Everett knew that there would be parties and meetings with Perry in the tents that night.

He was the last student to leave the field. One by one, his friends had gone. They had asked him to come with them, but he could only shake his head. It was Greta that had finally ushered them away.

The sun was setting when he finally stood up. His stiff joints protested, and his frozen hands reached up to clear away the last residue of his tears. He had come to a strange peace in the hours that he had sat alone in the field. He had seen the pain in his father's eyes in those final moments after the speech. Everett did not know what had happened between his mother and father, but he could see that a connection still existed, and it gave him a strange hope that he might someday come to know their story.

Mending

Everett was among the small crowd of students that waited on the hill the next morning to watch the astronaut leave. His eyes glittered with unshed tears as he silently wished his father well on his next mission, and then he turned away from the receding cars to go to his first class.

As he pulled his vehicle away from the school and set it to autopilot, Landon could only think about the boy with the hazel eyes. There had been something between him and the child, a connection that he did not understand.

Sighing, he pulled out the boy's file. A picture that had been taken of Everett on his testing day was on the cover, and he stared at the boy's long brown hair, round chin, and hazel eyes. Suddenly, he turned to look back at the school. The small crowd that had gathered to watch him leave was no longer visible. His heart thudded as he touched the picture with his finger.

Could it be? he wondered.

Everett resumed his former schedule feeling irrevocably changed by his brief interaction with his father and knew that he was better for it. He listened more closely to his instructors and tried to stop resisting their critique. Although their suggestions had made him defensive and impatient before, he could now see that his work only improved and evolved with each change. He knew that his father had worked hard on his goals and had achieved greatness because of it, and Everett wanted no less for himself.

After a week of awkward meals with Kimin, Sonniy, and Jeremiah, Everett asked his friends to meet him in his room. He knew that although his friends had started talking to one another again, they had never really aired their grievances, and their friendship was strained because of it. Kimin and Kabe were the most reluctant to agree to a group meeting. Kabe felt like everyone had already moved on, so there was no need to bring their argument back up, and Kimin was still a little angry and hurt.

In the end, they all showed up, and it felt very cramped once everyone was in Everett's room. After an awkward attempt at shuffling, Kabe suggested that they meet on a balcony at the end of the hallway. No one knew about the balcony except for Kabe, and he explained that there was a large covered balcony at the end of each dormitory hallway.

Everett noticed the door at the end of the hall for the first time and realized that he had never even looked down his hallway, and had definitely never explored it. Kabe's classwork seemed to be just as challenging as Everett's, and yet it seemed as though he did not struggle with managing his time the way that Everett did. He already knew so much about the school and had explored it more extensively than his friends had. Everett wondered if it was because they had different OVEREXCITABILITIES. The EMOTIONAL OE, which Kabe did not have, seemed to be the most taxing for Everett. His emotional response to thoughts about his parents always seemed to interfere with his ability to concentrate on his schoolwork.

Kabe pushed open the door that led to the balcony, and his friends spilled through the doorway behind him. There were both stationary and rocking chairs for them to sit in, in addition to outdoor tables and a hammock. Giggling, CiCi and Sonniy fell into the hammock together, so the others each grabbed a chair and pulled it over to face the hammock. Everett had been lucky to grab a rocking chair, and he gently rocked himself, enjoying the cool night breeze and the company of his friends.

The others seemed to sense the same peace that Everett felt, and the children fell silent as they watched the dusk slowly deepen into an inky darkness. Kabe remarked that there was no moon out that night, which startled the others away from their thoughts. Remembering why they were gathered, they looked around, wondering who would speak first.

"I'd like to start by apologizing," Kimin said quietly, looking down as she swirled her finger in circles on the arm of her chair. "I was frustrated when you all acted like my problem with Dre wasn't a big deal, when to me it is a big deal, and I said some mean things to you. I am sorry for that, but I lashed out because no one seemed to care about my problem."

Greta nodded and patted Kimin's shoulder to show that she accepted the apology.

"I know that you have the IMAGINATIONAL OVEREXCITABILITY Kimin," Greta said hesitantly. "Maybe you forgot that one of the characteristics of that OE is embellishing stories. I think that you got caught up in the drama of your situation and didn't want to hear the facts."

Kimin frowned and then nodded.

"Well, I also have the EMOTIONAL OE, so you all might think that I'm overreacting to something little, but to me it feels *big*. I also felt like you were judging me, Kabe, when you acted like I was just making everything up," Kimin shared, looking at Kabe through narrowed eyes.

Everett remembered the picture that he had drawn in his SKEtch pad about the EMOTIONAL OE, of the stick figure facing three other stick figures. He had drawn an arrow from the eyes of his stick figure to the faces of the other people to remind himself that he was more aware of how other people reacted to him. Remembering his picture helped him identify with what Kimin had experienced when they had all ignored her concern.

"I admit that I *did* feel like you were overreacting, Kimin, and I guess I don't understand how your OE makes you feel. I was viewing your situation from an objective, unemotional standpoint, so I wasn't judging you, I was just evaluating what made sense. It hurt my feelings when you implied that I was on Dre's side just because Jace is my cousin. I am also hurt that

Jeremiah doesn't want to talk to me anymore just because I hang out with Jace sometimes," Kabe added, looking from Kimin to Jeremiah. "Jace is my cousin, and I enjoy spending time with him. I don't ask you to hang out with me when I am with him because I know that you don't like him, but I also feel like you avoid me even when I'm not with him."

Jeremiah turned red at Kabe's words and shifted uncomfortably in his seat.

"Well, I felt like we were really good friends during our ORIENTATION, but now you only hang out with your cousin. You know that Jace and his friends bullied me, so I feel like you shouldn't spend time with him if you want to be my friend," Jeremiah rebutted nervously.

Kabe rocked back in his seat.

"Fine. Kimin was rude to me, so in order to be my friend, you have to choose between us. Kimin or me. I won't be your friend if you choose to continue to hang out with her, so make your choice," he told Jeremiah resolutely.

Kimin, Greta, and Jeremiah's jaws dropped, while Sonniy and CiCi sat up in the hammock, curious to find out what Jeremiah would say. Everett understood that Kabe was just trying to make Jeremiah understand how difficult it was to make choices between friends, but he was still curious to find out how Jeremiah would answer.

Jeremiah got out of his seat and paced for a few moments. He looked from Kabe, to Kimin, back to Kabe.

"I can't do that," he finally replied. "You are both my friends. I know that Kimin was wrong to force me to stop talking to you, but I still want to be friends with both of you."

Kimin squeaked a little and crossed her arms at Jeremiah's comment, but she still looked at Kabe curiously, wanting to know what his response would be.

"I don't really want you to choose between us Jeremiah," Kabe finally responded, sighing. "I just wanted you to see how it feels to have to choose between friends just because one of your friends doesn't like the other one. Just because *I* have a conflict with Kimin doesn't mean that I should force *you* not to be friends with her."

Jeremiah flushed.

"I understand now. I do want to be your friend, Kabe, but I would prefer to hang out with you when you are not with Jace. I won't hold it against you that you spend time with him anymore," Jeremiah replied, sounding chastised.

"*Do* you have a conflict with me Kabe?" Kimin asked in a small voice.

All eyes turned to look at Kabe. If he could not forgive Kimin, they might all be forced to choose sides again.

"Well, I don't like that I feel like everything has to be your way or you will get mad at me or not be my friend," Kabe responded bravely. All eyes moved to Kimin, anxious to hear her response.

"Okay, I understand what you mean Kabe. I regret that I said that I didn't want to be your friend anymore, and I guess I shouldn't have forced Sonniy and Jeremiah to go along with me when I did. I hate to feel like people aren't listening to me though, and I don't like it when people act like one of my problems isn't real. To me, a good friend always takes your side," she shot back.

All eyes shifted back to Kabe.

"I was *trying* to show you another viewpoint," he replied through clenched teeth. "You can't *always* be right Kimin. It is possible, just possible, that everything you said that the *originals* did to you was *coincidental.*"

"Yes," she replied, sounding just as irritated, "but it is also possible that it was *intentional.* Based on our history with the *originals*, I say that the latter is more likely. I know that you stood up to them during your ORIENTATION, so you feel like the problem with them has been resolved, but I wasn't with you all when that happened, so the problem has not been resolved for me."

Kabe closed his mouth as he considered her words.

"I understand your point Kimin. It makes sense, and I apologize for assuming that our situations with the *originals* are the same. I still think, though, that you have a hard time listening to other viewpoints," he said slowly, looking at her to gauge her reaction.

She crossed her arms, but her expression was thoughtful.

"Okay, I can agree with you about that," she replied as a slow smile spread across her face and a twinkle crept into her eyes.

The other children laughed with relief, and after some playful shoulder shoving and laughter, it seemed as though order had been restored to the small, fragile group of children. Everett knew that they were all so unused to belonging to a group of friends and that they would each make mistakes as they learned to understand and support each other. Perry's words echoed in his mind as he watched his friends talk and laugh.

Most of all, though, I forgot to thank my friends. The friends that listened to me talk for hours about my problems, about my plans, and about my dreams. The friends that put aside their work on days that I needed someone to spend time with. The friends that brought me gently back to reality when I needed it and pushed me beyond my limits when I needed that. So take the time to be a friend, to help a friend, and to enjoy your friends. Most of all, throughout the years, don't forget to thank your friends.

Spontaneously, surprising himself and his friends, Everett abandoned his usual reserve and stood up to hug each of them in turn. He knew that the words to thank them would come to him in time, but for now, this gesture would have to be enough.

Taking Control

Everett sat up in bed the following morning feeling tired but at peace. He had stayed up for most of the night, reflecting on his days at the SFGP and thinking about his future there. Landon Perry's words had drifted through his mind as he considered his brief experience at the school. So far, he had taken very little control over his learning. He felt like a bottle trapped in a turbulent sea, allowing himself to be carried along, this way and that, as he received direction from others.

He was ambivalent about the earth science class that he was enrolled in. Although he had learned a lot of interesting information in the class, and it had helped him understand how to create a good soil mixture for his plant experiment, it just was not engaging him the way that his other science class did.

Listening to Landon Perry speak so passionately about the school and how it had helped him reach his full POTENTIAL had caused Everett to realize that he wanted the same thing. He did not want to just be at the school and take the classes that they assigned to him. He realized that he did have goals, and interests, and that he wanted to take full advantage of what the school had to offer him.

Being at this school may not have been my choice, but I can take control of what I do while I am here, he had decided at some point in the night.

Gathering his courage, he sent a video message to Mr. Dodd to request a meeting. It was the students' day of rest, so he was not sure if Mr. Dodd would be available. He was thankful when he received Mr. Dodd's startled response agreeing to meet with him in half an hour. Everett forced a strained smile and ordered a small breakfast. He was almost too nervous to eat, but he knew that his body needed the nourishment.

He arrived in Mr. Dodd's classroom early. The room was empty, and a mixture of emotions washed through him as he entered. He had experienced so much in this classroom, had grown to know so much about himself, and had built friendships for the first time in his life in there. A tear slipped down his cheek as the memories flowed through him.

"Good morning Everett," Mr. Dodd said kindly, trying not to startle him. "To what do I owe this honor?"

Everett looked up at Mr. Dodd with a shy smile and took the seat that his former instructor offered him.

"Well, I have some questions that I'd like to ask, and I might want to make some changes to my schedule. Since I no longer have Sindra to advise me, I was hoping that you would," Everett told him.

Mr. Dodd nodded and pursed his lips.

"Yes, I have long been an advocate for our students to continue to have a mentor throughout their studies, rather than just during their ORIENTATION, but the Chancellor and I have a difference of opinion on the subject. I would be happy to help you. Tell me your concerns," Mr. Dodd replied, leaning forward with interest.

Everett raised his eyebrows. Another instructor expressing dislike for The School for Gifted Potentials? He thought it was interesting that Ms. Rosenthal and Mr. Dodd had both been mentioned in Landon Perry's speech, so both had been instructors at the SFGP *before* Chancellor Grey had taken control of the school.

"Well, I have two science classes in my schedule," Everett started, frowning as he searched for the words to explain his problem. "At first I was really excited, because I have always dreamed about being allowed to study science all day, but I guess I'm not as interested in earth science as I thought I was. The life science class is great, and in fact, I realize that there is a lot more to that subject than I even thought possible. I'm actually starting to like the technical writing class as well, even though it is my area of weakness. I am learning so much about how to express my thinking and it really is helping me create better experimental designs."

Everett trailed off, searching for his question.

Mr. Dodd waited patiently as Everett struggled to think through his problem. It had seemed so clear the night before, but now he could not seem to express it aloud to Mr. Dodd.

"Well, I guess this school is all about POTENTIAL, and I feel like maybe my POTENTIAL isn't fully being tapped into. When I am in the earth science class, I feel like I am learning, but I don't feel like I am *growing*. I want to know what my other options are, so that all of my classes help me reach my full POTENTIAL," he finally shared, pulling together his scattered thoughts.

"Hmm. That is a remarkable observation. You have not been at our school for very long, so I could encourage you to give your earth science class one more chance, or I could encourage you to change your topic of study within that class," Mr. Dodd said lightly. "But I think that instead I will trust your observations and help you consider some other possibilities. I hope that you have already considered your other areas of STRENGTH and that you have an idea about what your replacement class could be."

Everett nodded eagerly.

"Well, I have always loved math. In fact, slipping up and showing my STRENGTH in math is how I got caught by an Observer. I know that I *use* math in my science classes, but I really just want to learn math as a subject, like my friend Jeremiah does. I remember that my test scores showed that I have a SPECIFIC ACADEMIC APTITUDE in math, so I think that it makes sense to make it one of my classes," Everett said, peeking up at Mr. Dodd hopefully.

He chose not to add that he had looked through Landon Perry's autobiography to find out what his schedule had been in his early years at the SFGP and had found out that Landon had studied math along with life science.

Mr. Dodd was silent for a long time, but Everett did not know that it was because he was considering Everett's comment about being "caught" by an Observer. It was a strange way to view being selected as a candidate for the school. As far as Mr. Dodd knew, with his limited access to the world outside of the school, being selected to test at The School for Gifted Potentials was considered an honor.

"Tell me more about what the Observer saw that prompted her to test you," he said, wanting to understand more of Everett's story. "It might give me some insight into what class to place you in."

Everett flushed and swung his feet under the chair. It seemed that the secrets of his past continued to make him feel like he had to lie to people that were only trying to help him. Suddenly he wondered what it would feel like if he told Mr. Dodd the reason that he was at the school. He could not imagine that his kind instructor would use the information to harm him.

"Well, my mother never wanted me to come here," he started slowly, deciding to trust his instructor. "I worked really hard when I was growing up to hide my STRENGTHS, my sensitivities, and my interests. My mother taught me how to act like the other children at my school, taught me how to get involved in their activities, and told me not to show what I could really do in class. One day, though, an Observer came to my classroom and pretended to be a replacement teacher."

Everett frowned, struggling with the memory.

"She worked with me on patterns and then showed me a counting system that I had never seen before."

Everett's throat closed for a moment, and he pushed himself off of his chair to stand at the window. The words rushed through him now, eager to be freed.

"I knew that I shouldn't have shown her that I understood her pattern, but it felt so amazing to do something so challenging at school. My mother and I always did great things together at home. She let me read books that were at my level, she taught me math strategies, and we did lots of science experiments together. But that was only for a little while each night, and I wanted to learn all day, every day."

Everett's voice squeaked as he came to a realization.

"So you see, it's *my* fault that I am here. *I* made the mistake. I've been blaming my mother for leaving me here, but I was the one that broke our agreement, not her," he whispered, a great sob shaking his shoulders. It both hurt and healed him to acknowledge that part of his pain over his mother's abandonment stemmed from the guilt that he still felt for interacting with the Observer.

"You have *every* right to want to learn," Mr. Dodd said softly, standing just behind Everett. "In fact, you *need* to learn. It was very clear during your ORIENTATION that you have the INTELLECTUAL OVEREXCITABILITY. You should not be ashamed of your need and desire to know more, to explore and discover, to consider possibilities. You want to be fully engrossed in your learning throughout your day, so I agree that we should find you a better class. I will review your test data, and you should receive a video message sometime next week letting you know what your new class will be."

Everett turned to face him with a sniff and pulled in a shuddering, renewing breath of air. They both settled back into their chairs. Mr. Dodd hoped that his face did not show his surprise about what the boy had revealed. It was the first time that he had ever heard of a student trying to stay out of the school. It seemed like the students were usually so eager to attend. Of course, many were sad and struggled with feelings of loss over leaving their families, but none had ever gone out of their way to avoid the attention of an Observer, at least none that he knew about.

"With the EMOTIONAL OVEREXCITABILITY, it must be difficult for you to deal with these emotions," Mr. Dodd prompted him after a while, sensing that he had more issues to resolve.

Everett sat with his elbows on his knees and his head hung low on his shoulders. He bobbed his head slightly to show his agreement with Mr. Dodd's statement before he looked up.

"Yeah, it has been really hard. I guess I kind of feel like it is wrong for me to like my classes and my friends so much. My mother and I had a very clear plan; that we would always be together, that I would never attend this school. I have been so angry with her for leaving me here, but I have also been enjoying it, so I feel kind of guilty," Everett said as he shoved his head into his hands in frustration. "It feels like, every time I make some progress, some feeling overwhelms me and drags me down!"

Mr. Dodd nodded and placed a hand on Everett's shoulder.

"Your EMOTIONAL OVEREXCITABILITY is working in two ways here Everett, although I think that you only see the negative side of your feelings right now. Please remember that we discussed both sides of every OE during your ORIENTATION, to understand that although the OEs can cause pain or frustration at times, they can also help you experience the world in wondrous ways. You clearly have a deep connection to your mother, and you have developed a connection with several of your friends. Both of these emotional attachments are positive, and you should not view having more than one attachment as choosing sides. You can love your mother, and your friends, without feeling disloyal to either side. You have a great capacity for caring, in many ways, for all different kinds of people. Do you feel like your new friendships have helped you grow or change in any way?" Mr. Dodd asked, his eyes searching Everett's for signs of understanding.

Everett stretched and twisted in his chair as he considered Mr. Dodd's question.

Of course, I have grown. I have only ever had my mother to care about before coming here. I love her so much, but now I am finding that I have room in my heart for more than just one person. Maybe that is why this is so painful.

To Mr. Dodd he said, "Yeah, I guess I just have to get used to having more people to care about and worry about now that I'm here. My friends are all so different, and I have to approach each of them in a different way so that I don't upset them. That is a new experience for me. My mother and I were so honest with each other. I never had to worry that she would stop liking me or stop talking to me if she got mad at me."

Hot tears coursed down his cheeks again, surprising him. He had not realized how much Kimin's rejection had hurt him until that moment. He angrily tried to dash the tears from his face with the backs of his hands, but they continued to flow profusely. As if a dam had burst loose, he let himself cry until the sobs slowly subsided. Unlike the tears that he had shed during his ORIENTATION, which had left him feeling drained, these tears seemed to release some of the stress that had built up inside of him, and he felt renewed.

"Yes, I do think that I have grown, and I've learned a lot about making friends, but I also know that I'm going to keep on making mistakes," Everett finally shared.

Mr. Dodd motioned for Everett to follow him out of the classroom. His patient silence reassured Everett that their time was not over yet, and the movement and the change of setting calmed his churning stomach. He took a deep breath and tried to refocus on his reasons for meeting with Mr. Dodd.

"It is interesting that you mentioned making mistakes," Mr. Dodd finally said. "In the world outside of the SFGP, mistakes are often viewed as a bad thing, something to avoid, and sometimes something to be ashamed of. Here, within these walls, I believe that we *encourage* our students to make mistakes. Would it be better to have never tried making friends, so that you never had to make a mistake? Or is it better to have made friends, even though you made a few mistakes along the way?"

Everett nodded to show that he would rather have his friends and was rewarded with a smile.

"You have already learned so much about being a friend because you made mistakes and learned from them. It is the same with your science experiment, which was most impressive by the way. In your narrative, when you made a change, you didn't try to hide it or cover up the fact that you changed something. You acknowledged the error, the reasons for it, and the changes that you made to correct it," Mr. Dodd continued.

"Of course I did, because that's what science *is*. You are *experimenting*, so of course things won't always go exactly the way you planned," Everett protested, wondering what point Mr. Dodd was trying to make.

"So why don't you give yourself permission to make mistakes in all areas of your life, the way that you do for science?" Mr. Dodd asked, looking at Everett out of the corner of his eye.

Everett stopped walking and faced Mr. Dodd. A slow smile spread across his face as his instructor's message sank in, and he impulsively hugged Mr. Dodd's midsection.

"Thank you Mr. Dodd. That is just what I think I will do."

Accepting Failure

Everett hurried to his INTENSIVE the next day with a light, carefree step. He had finally been assigned to a MUSIC class. Greta had enjoyed learning the basics of how to play a flute, and Sonniy had impressed him with her cello, so he was excited to find out if he would have a STRENGTH in MUSIC as well.

As he walked into the classroom, he saw that it was a huge space with instruments displayed on every wall. A multitude of stools were available to sit on, and each stool had a tall stand in front of it. He settled onto one of the empty stools and looked up. A magnificent glass ceiling loomed overhead, several stories above him, and he watched the clouds pass overhead for a long time. He was so caught up in the view that he did not notice the students that trickled slowly into the classroom.

The loud voice of the instructor speaking over the din of chatting students finally pulled his attention back to his surroundings, and he was startled to see bodies sitting on each of the stools. He studied the other students' faces surreptitiously, searching for *originals* in the classroom.

A sigh of relief escaped him when he did not recognize a single other face. His vow to make mistakes without worrying about what others thought of him would be easier without an *original* watching him.

The instructor informed the class that they would spend some time at the beginning of the class to find out which instrument suited their mouth shape the best. A robot appeared to pass out a tray of mouthpieces to each student. Everett suddenly felt as though his teacher was speaking a foreign language as she demonstrated how to use each one, but he fumbled his way through the process.

He tested out all of the mouthpieces, surprised at the strange sensation that he felt when he blew through each one, and by how difficult it was to make each one create a sound. He was somewhat breathless when the instructor finally told them all to pause.

She asked the students to wave their hands over the screen on the stand in front of them. He was surprised to see that the stand was like a SKEtch pad with a vertical support. As he waved his hand, a video appeared.

The video showed different Gifted Potentials explaining how to read music notes. The instructor went to each student individually to help them determine which instrument would suit them best as the other students watched the video on their screen.

Everett was startled when she finally appeared at his side because he was so engrossed in the video. She waved her hand over the screen, which paused the video, and smiled kindly at him.

"Hello Everett. I would like for you to blow into each of these mouthpieces for me so that I can help you determine which one will work best for you," she said, motioning to the tray on his lap.

He flushed but bravely picked up each mouthpiece in turn and blew into it. She corrected the way that he blew into several of them, and showed him how to tighten his lips to make a sound come out for some, and how to control his breathing on others.

A relieved laugh escaped him as he realized that he had made mistakes on just about every mouthpiece, but his stomach had not dropped with anxiety over it, not even once.

"How do you feel?" she asked kindly, cocking her head to the side as she waited for his answer.

"Tired," he admitted with a small laugh, causing her to laugh in turn. "The muscles in my cheeks hurt a little and I'm not sure I will remember which mouthpiece needed me to blow into it which way, but I am still excited to learn how to play something."

She grinned and tapped the mouthpiece for the clarinet. "I think that you should learn to play the clarinet today. Once I have finished meeting with everyone, I will bring the rest of the instrument to you. You can wave your hand over the screen when you are ready to resume the video."

The instructor marked something on her SKEtch pad and moved over to the next student. He grinned, wondering what a clarinet was, and waved his hand over the screen. The students on the video broke down each music note and explained it and even played the notes on various instruments. Despite their clear instruction, Everett found that he still did not understand most of what they were saying. He was impressed by his friend Sonniy's ability to read music so well and humbled by his difficulty with learning it.

Once the instructor had finished meeting with each student, she gave each student an instrument and showed them how to put the mouthpiece on. The instrument that she handed him was covered in holes and had shiny metal keys projecting off of it. He grinned as he followed her directions and put the mouthpiece on the instrument.

For the rest of the class period, he tried to play a simple tune that his instructor had assigned to him. Once each student had set up their instruments, they received an individualized instructional video for the instrument that they held. Everett was only able to make several squeaks and one note in the time that they had to practice, and he shook his head and shrugged at his instructor as he handed his instrument back to her.

"This is not a natural talent for me, but I did have fun," he told her honestly.

"Are you interested in receiving some individualized instruction? Some of our advanced students give private lessons," she offered and rested her hip on his stand while she waited for him to respond.

His immediate reaction was to agree, but just as he was about to accept her offer, the thought that the advanced student might be an *original* crossed his mind.

Hesitantly, he nodded, but asked, "If the student that volunteers to help me is someone that I have a problem with, can I request a different tutor?"

She frowned as she tried to figure out his meaning. He kept his face blank, hoping that she would not probe for more information, and she finally shrugged.

"Of course. I will have a student contact you to help you learn the clarinet sometime next week. I was glad to have you in my INTENSIVE, and please feel free to sign up for this class again," she said as she straightened and moved on to the next student.

Everett received a video message that night that instructed him to attend a seminar the following day. He squinted as he reviewed the seminar's location on the attached map and felt a thrill when he realized that he had never been to that section of the school before. Out of curiosity, he called Greta to see if she was going to the seminar as well, since she had been at the last one.

"Yes, I just got the message," she replied and shook her head. "What do you think it will be about?"

"I don't know," he replied, and then shrugged. "I guess we'll find out together. How was your INTENSIVE today?"

She shrugged.

"I don't know. Learning to play the flute and the basics of ballet suited me perfectly, but today I went to a class that was all about thinking freely. We got a bunch of abstract pictures made out of lines and shapes, and we had to come up with a bunch of different ideas about what they could be. The instructor kept telling us that there was no right answer and that it was better to have lots of spontaneous ideas than one well thought out idea, but I really struggled with that concept."

He nodded, knowing that her need to be perfect and her fear of being judged had probably played a role in her reluctance to participate.

"To make it worse, Jace and Dre were in the class. Jace was actually pretty nice to me, I think because he has seen me with Kabe before, but Dre was really competitive. She was in the group next to me, but she kept looking over at me when she was giving answers. It was obvious that it wasn't her first time in that INTENSIVE, but she kept bragging about her speed anyway," Greta shared, making an uncharacteristic face about the *original's* behavior.

Everett chuckled and shook his head.

"I got to take a MUSIC INTENSIVE," he shared. "I know that you really enjoyed it, and I was excited about it, but it's clear that playing an instrument and reading music do not come easily to me. The thing is though; I was finally okay with that today. I set a goal to start being more comfortable with making mistakes after a talk that I had with Mr. Dodd. He pointed out that I don't mind making mistakes in science, because I understand that making mistakes is part of designing an experiment, so he said that I should approach everything that I do with the same attitude. I tried that today and it really worked, although it helped that there weren't any *originals* in my class."

Greta leaned forward, her face lit up by a new understanding.

"What an amazing way to look at making mistakes," she said. "I don't mind making mistakes in science, because I know that they are part of the process, but I hate making mistakes in everything else. I never thought about why I am comfortable making mistakes in science, but I can see the connection now. This really helps!"

Everett nodded and then waited for a sign from Greta that their conversation could continue. Their conversation had already been longer than most, and he wanted to give her the chance to get back to her work if she needed to.

"You know, my parents said that it was hard to be a G and make mistakes," Greta continued, taking Everett by surprise.

It was his turn to lean forward with interest.

"Really? Why was it hard to be a G?" he asked with genuine interest.

"Well, I guess people assume that once you have the G, and you have mastered your field of study, that you must be the best at everything. People seemed to expect more out of my parents because of the G, even when the activity had nothing to do with their area of STRENGTH," she shared with a frown.

"What do you mean?" he asked, unable to relate to what she was talking about because his mother had never gotten her tattoo.

"Well, one time my parents went to a colleague's apartment for dinner. He was not a G and neither was his wife. When the meal was over, they asked my parents to play a game of cards with them. The other couple won the game several times, and my mother said that the couple kept on making remarks when my parents lost, like they were so surprised that they could beat a G," she said, sneering to match the tone of the couple in the story. "When they got home, my mother was upset. She said 'it's not as if we earned the G in *card games*', and my father just shrugged. People just expect them to be great all the time, at everything. I don't think that's fair."

Greta frowned, and Everett shook his head. His mother had never taken the G tattoo, and he wondered if that had made life easier for her. The symbol earned the owner a lot of respect, but it seemed to have a negative side as well. He wondered if his former classmates would treat him differently if he went back to school wearing his Gifted Potential uniform.

"That's a lot to think about," he finally said.

"Yeah," she responded, wrinkling her nose.

A long silence stretched between them as both children thought about what life might hold after The School for Gifted Potentials and what it might be like to have the G. Everett wished that he could talk to Landon Perry about what it was like to be a G, a famous one, and to ask him about the pressures that came with being legendary.

"I'd better get back to work now. I'll see you at the seminar tomorrow," Greta finally said, reluctantly breaking their mutual silence.

He nodded as she smiled softly and waved farewell.

After the screen went blank, Everett pulled up his brain bridge to write about his INTENSIVE. He flushed when he realized that he had never reflected on his freshwater ecology INTENSIVE because he had been so upset by the call from Landon Perry.

He created a freshwater ecology section and then zoomed in to describe it. Overall, he had enjoyed the experience and had learned a lot about gathering live samples to view later in a laboratory. Everett wrote a quick summary of the experience and was about to switch to his MUSIC INTENSIVE when he recalled the strange conversation that he'd had with Ms. Rosenthal in front of the POD.

A chill of misgiving crept through him as he wondered why she had let him know that she did not approve of everything at The School for Gifted Potentials. She knew that he was not exactly happy about being at the school because he had made it very clear at his first meeting with her that he did not belong there, so he wondered why she was not trying to change his mind about the school.

What had she been trying to influence him to do?

Sighing, he wrote a large R to represent Rosenthal and then drew a circle of question marks surrounding it so that he would remember that he still had questions about her meaning. He did not write a summary of their interaction, though, suddenly wondering if his SKEtch pad files were completely private.

Trying to push the strange encounter out of his mind, Everett created a MUSIC section next and zoomed in to add the details of his most recent INTENSIVE. He drew a clarinet and labeled the parts that he had learned, the mouthpiece and the keys, then jotted down what he remembered about reading music and grimaced when he realized that he did not remember very much.

His greatest accomplishment in the class had been allowing himself to make some mistakes. It surprised him that he had not felt his stomach drop or his heart race with anxiety over messing up, not even once. He understood that it would not be easy to pull that attitude into everything that he did, but he was glad that the strategy had helped him get through at least that class.

Underneath his music sketches, he drew a picture of himself holding up a shield, thinking about how he used to try to protect himself from criticism, and then drew lines coming through the shield to show that the criticism got through anyway. Next to it, he drew himself standing with open arms, as if he was welcoming the criticism, and then drew only a few lines piercing through him as the other lines went past him, to show that when he expected the criticism, it felt like he received a lot less.

Feeling restless, he scrolled through the other files on his SKEtch pad to review what he had accomplished in his few short weeks at the school and found a picture that he had started and given up on. He had decided to draw a picture of his visualization of the moths in the meadow. He had tried to capture the image with his stylus on his SKEtch pad, but had only been able to create a flat picture with no sense of sentiment in it.

On an impulse, he decided to call CiCi.

"Hi Everett!" she squeaked, sounding genuinely surprised and happy that he had called her.

"Hey CiCi. I have been trying to draw a picture on my SKEtch pad, but I just can't get it right. I'm hoping that you can give me some advice," he said.

"Oh, okay. I have time right now if you want to start right away. We could meet at my drawing studio," she offered.

He nodded and agreed to meet her there. It had not taken long for the faculty to realize what Everett had always noticed, that CiCi had a STRENGTH in VISUAL ARTS. He imagined that her drawing studio would be much like Sonniy's practice studio and his laboratory, and he eagerly walked toward it. She was waiting for him at the door to her studio, practically quivering with excitement.

"Hey Everett," she said with her dimpled grin. "I am so happy to help you. Thanks for asking!"

She waved her badge in front of a sensor, and Everett was shocked when the door opened. He had expected to find a drawing table and some supplies, but what he found was wall-to-wall color. There were words in different sizes and fonts plastered among pencil sketches, watercolor paintings, and oil paintings.

His mouth was agape when their eyes met, and she laughed gleefully in response. She waved a hand in front of the wall facing the door, and the clutter of art instantly disappeared and was replaced by a white wall. The other two walls remained covered with words and pieces of art. He realized that her walls were giant screens like the wall in Ms. Everlay's office.

"That's just a digital collection of my some of my work," she explained airily. "One of the things that I'm working on right now is finding things that inspire me to create my artwork."

She waved her hand again, and the image of a dark forest thick with moss appeared. A single tree was featured, its ancient roots twisting and winding through the dirt around the base of the tree. She waved again, and a dancer replaced the forest. The dancer was swathed in black and twirled across a stage that resembled a dragon's back. CiCi shrugged at this image and waved again. The screen showed a white balloon floating gently on a breeze.

"Those are really interesting," he told her encouragingly.

She waved again, and a night sky that glittered with stars replaced the balloon.

"This is the one that I use the most. I try the other ones every once in a while, but they haven't really worked for me yet. A MASTERY student gave them to me from her own collection. She spent over a decade collecting videos and images that inspire her, and she said that I would need to invest the same amount of time in finding my own. It is kind of like the visualization technique that we learned in Mr. Dodd's class. Everyone kind of has to find what works for them," she said with a shrug.

His young friend's insight and composure continued to amaze him, and he smiled as he reached out to tug affectionately on a lock of her hair.

"Well, it's interesting that you mentioned that, because my visualization is exactly what I've been trying to draw. I have been using a particular image when I visualize, but even though I can conjure up the image in my mind, I think that I would also like to have a copy of it to look at. I just can't get it right though," he shared, some of his frustration with the process creeping into his voice.

"Tell me about what you are picturing," she said encouragingly.

She sprang off of her stool and stood in front of a set of drawers that were built into her table. After a moment of consideration, she grabbed a sheet of paper and a pencil, and then looked up at him to show that she was ready to listen.

"Well, there is a field. The sun is just beginning to set over the mountains, so there is golden light shooting through everything. I am standing in these tall, wispy grasses that reach up to my waist. Suddenly, these little white moths flutter up out

~ 138 ~

of the grasses and surround me. It almost felt like they were aware of me, like they were greeting me in a way, and then they were gone. The sun sank lower, and I had to leave to get back to the POD before it got dark. But that moment has stayed with me ever since," he shared, his voice dropping off as he lost himself in the memory once again.

CiCi nodded at his story. He had been careful to leave his mother out of the story, but he could tell that she had gathered the mood of the moment anyway.

He grabbed his SKEtch pad and pulled up the picture that he had started. She nodded and told him that he needed to shade his drawing. He frowned to show that he did not understand what she meant, so she drew a quick sketch of him standing in the grasses and then showed him how to use the edge of a pencil to make some of the grasses look as though they were illuminated by light, while others were cast into shadow. He sucked in his breath at the effect that she had been able to create. CiCi pulled colored pencils out of her drawers that matched the setting that he had described and grabbed several large sheets of drawing paper. She pushed them toward him encouragingly and then jumped onto her stool to work on her own piece of art.

He spent a few moments visualizing the scene before he picked up his pencil. When inspiration struck, he snatched up a fresh sheet of paper and quickly sketched out the scene, then spent the remainder of his time practicing the shading technique that she had taught him. He experimented with the different colors that she had given him and then shyly asked if he could rummage through her supplies to find other colors. She nodded happily as she opened a drawer for him and then turned on the sound of a rushing river for them to work to. He felt completely relaxed in her environment.

He finally showed her his best attempt at shading, and she rewarded him with her sweet smile.

"This must be a special memory. I can tell by the way you shaded it," she said softly.

"Yeah, it is," he replied, looking at her sideways. As always, he was impressed by her perceptiveness. She seemed much older than her size allowed. "How old are you, anyway?"

"Six," she responded with a dimpled grin. "I'm halfway to being seven though."

"You just seem so much older," he told her, hoping that his observation would not offend her.

"Oh, that's because of my ASYNCHRONY," she said with a shrug and hopped off her stool to grab some clay.

"Your what?" he asked.

He had never heard the word before.

"ASYNCHRONY, you know, where you can have a different body age, mental age, and emotional age," she said as she jumped back up on her stool.

She laughed when she saw his puzzled look.

"Okay, so my body is six, but my mind works like an eight-year-old, and I have the emotions of a nine-year-old. That's why I seem so mature. Another person with ASYNCHRONY could have the body of a six-year-old, the mind of a ten-year-old, and the emotions of a four-year-old. I went to a seminar about it," she said, cocking her head to one side as she concentrated on stretching out her clay.

Everett frowned as he considered her words. Which was he? Were his emotions ahead of his age, the same, or behind? He considered how he had coped with everything that had happened since he had turned ten. His worst nightmare had happened. He had been summoned to The School for Gifted Potentials, and the mother that he had always trusted had left him behind. He was now living alone, surrounded by strangers, a few friends, robots, instructors, originals, and the Chancellor.

He thought that he was coping well, although maybe he should be coping better. Was he handling the situation the way that another child his age would? Was he handling it better than expected? Worse? Now he was not sure. He wondered why he had not been invited to a seminar about ASYNCHRONY.

He sighed, knowing that there was still so much for him to figure out about his new life.

"Well, thanks for your help CiCi," he said earnestly as he got off his stool. He hugged her around the shoulders and walked back to his room, grateful that he had such talented and caring friends.

A Clever Coup

The Chancellor sat in his office, staring blankly at the wall. A strange feeling pricked the back of his neck, and he swiveled his chair around to look at the door.

"Camilla," he said dryly. She stood in his doorway with her shoulder resting on the doorframe and her arms crossed over her chest.

"Well, come in," he said slowly.

She remained in the doorway for a moment, then pushed off of the frame and moved to the chair across from him. They stared at each other for a while, neither wanting to be the first to break the tense silence. He sat back in his chair, knowing that she had come to confront him and would not be able to wait to speak much longer. He had not seen his sister for over a decade. She looked better, and worse.

"Well," she finally said. "How are things at the SFGP?"

Her insolent tone did not bother him. They had always had a strained relationship.

"It is wonderful," he replied as if she had been sincere. "Landon was just here. He has risen to a level of fame that I believe none of us had thought possible. It was wonderful to show the students what can be accomplished by those with the G."

She knew that he was pointing out Landon's G tattoo to hurt her. When she had completed her MASTERY program, her brother had just become the Chancellor. He had immediately changed the residency requirements at the school to make it mandatory to live there and had cut off all visits with family. She had known that his personal prejudices were the reason for the change and had tried to persuade her friends to refuse the G tattoo to protest the new rule along with her.

She had expected Landon to protest with her. They had been friends since she had started at The School for Gifted Potentials.

Landon was in her ORIENTATION class and had started a few days earlier than her. She had been five and he had been eight, and he had taken her under his wing immediately. The close friendship that had started when they were children had grown into a relationship as they got older, and Landon had swiftly become the most important person in her life.

They had secretly married each other the night that they completed their MASTERY studies and had planned to announce their marriage to their friends on the day that they received their tattoos, just after the graduation ceremony, before they left the school to work together in Asia.

When she had asked Landon to support her objection to her brother's rule by refusing the tattoo along with her, he had said that he didn't agree with the new residency rule either, but he also did not believe that their protest would reverse her brother's decision. He argued that he had worked his entire life to earn the G and wanted the opportunities that it would afford him.

She had been shocked that he would not support her and had not attended the ceremony when he and their friends had gotten their tattoos. She left the school the following morning to get some space from her husband, too angry with him to see him for a while. To her surprise and disappointment, he did not try to find her. She had discovered her pregnancy a few months later.

When she had contacted him to make amends and tell him about the pregnancy, he had announced that he had entered the space program before she could share the news. He had explained that it was an enormous commitment and that he would be unavailable throughout the training program so that he could focus on everything that he needed to learn.

His news had been quite a blow to her, but she understood that it was something that he would love, and she knew that he would make a great astronaut. She had decided not to share the news of her pregnancy with him. They were no longer in the same loving relationship that they had been in, and she was afraid that if he left the space program for her, he would resent her for it. She also knew that if she told him about the child, and he decided to move forward with his training anyway, that it would destroy her. It was best to let him move on without her, she had decided, and they had not spoken since.

She jolted herself away from her thoughts, regretting that she had given her brother the chance to see that his words had gotten to her.

"Yes, Landon has done very well for himself," she replied with a careless shrug. "So have you, *Chancellor*. I did not expect you to keep your position this long."

He raised his eyebrows at her comment, but did not respond to her goading.

"I see that you have not changed your residency policy," she continued, looking him in the eye. "You are *still* forcing parents to make a terrible choice. They either have to give up their child forever so that they can have an appropriate education, or they have to force their child to suffer through schooling that does nothing for them just so they can hold their child each night. Why do you think that it's fair for you to *force* them to make that choice?"

"Children that traveled back and forth between this school and their homes often struggled with the differences between their two worlds," he began, launching into his familiar lecture about the value of full-time residency.

"You mean that *you* struggled to go back and forth," she interrupted angrily.

She knew that his reasons for requiring residency were tainted by his own experiences.

His face clouded. This was the only topic that could shake his cool exterior. His sister was the only one that knew what his childhood had been like, and he hated that she knew his secrets.

"You know what it was like for me," he hissed. "Here, I was admired, encouraged, and valued. My instructors and my friends supported me. Our father…" He trailed off. Going home had been difficult for him. Their father had been a hard man to please. "Our father looked at me in a different way. He always wanted *more* from me; he always wanted me to be *different*. Whenever I told him about my OVEREXCITABILITIES, he saw them as excuses. He did not accept me the way that my instructors did. They always pointed out my STRENGTHS; Father always pointed out my weaknesses. I always wondered what my life would have been like if I had grown up here, if I had only ever had a positive view of myself. That is what I want for my students."

"*You* commuted back and forth from school to home, but *I* never got that chance," Camilla retorted. "Unlike you, I had a good relationship with our father. He was quiet and reserved, but we had a wonderful relationship. When my mother died, he said that his grief was too great for him to be a proper caretaker for me. You had badgered him enough about the positive side of living here full-time, so he decided to enroll *both* of us as full-time students. You were ecstatic about the news, but I lost both of my parents in a matter of a few weeks."

They glared at each other for a moment before she continued.

"You thought that living here full-time was paradise, but it was harder for me. If I had been able to go home and visit Father whenever I needed to, I would not have felt so lost and alone here. The education that I received at this school was phenomenal, and I made many wonderful friends, but I missed having a *family*. It is not right that you force parents to give up their children just so that they have the chance to learn. They should have the *choice!*" she said, and banged her fist on his desk at the last word, causing him to jump.

He smoothed his goatee uncomfortably.

"Well, I made that choice for my own daughter. She started here at the age of six months, and I have to say that she is doing very well. She excels in every area and is very secure emotionally. I cannot imagine that I could have done a better job," he told her proudly.

"Yes, I know that you enrolled your daughter here as an infant. I also heard that you visit with her almost every day. My friends told me that Diedre and her friends get a lot of special attention from you. It is easy for you to say that it does not hurt to send your child here, because you have not had to be without her. You can see her any time you want!" she retorted, crossing her arms as she leaned back in her chair.

He was silent. His sister had made a good point, and he had no way to defend himself from it. He had never really looked at the situation in that way. It shook him a little to realize that it was true that he had found a way around his own rules, to have his daughter enrolled in the school and also see her any time that he wanted to.

"So you see, brother, once again your judgment has been clouded by your experiences," Camilla continued, realizing that she had her brother at a disadvantage. "Because *you* had a difficult childhood, you assume that everyone else will have one as well. Because you had an easy time putting your daughter here as an infant, you imagine that your sacrifice is the same as everyone else's, when in reality, you have not really had to give her up at all."

She rose out of her chair slowly.

"I want a position as an instructor," she said, staring him in the eye.

His brows rose in surprise. He could not have imagined that she would want to work at the school when she was so adamantly against his policy.

"Fine. I have just received notice that a science instructor is taking a leave of absence to conduct research in the field. I will give you a six-month contract to take her place while she is gone.

I hope that you will enjoy being back," he said with a mocking smile.

She turned on her heel and walked out of his office, hiding a triumphant smile as she left.

Everett followed the directions on his map to a new section of the school to find his seminar, wondering what the topic was, and on some level, worrying that it meant that he was lacking in some area. Although Mr. Dodd had reassured Greta that being in a seminar did not mean that a student had done something wrong, he had not been to enough of them to completely trust that.

A shiver ran down his back as he wondered if Mr. Dodd would be there for the seminar, and he hurried down the hallway. It was in a section of the school that he had not been to before, and he took a wrong turn before finding the room.

As he scanned his badge and walked into the room, he realized that it was more of an auditorium than a classroom. A quick scan of the room showed that it had tiers of seating that led down to a large platform. Instead of chairs, large pillows were scattered along the tiers. The room was about halfway full, and Everett suddenly felt intimidated. This was not the intimate environment that Mr. Dodd had created at his last seminar.

His stomach dropped as he scanned the room for a place to sit, and as he moved down a few steps to a tier in the middle, he nearly tripped over Kabe. They shared a surprised grin, and Everett settled next to Kabe on a soft foam pillow.

He noticed a variety of small wooden puzzles scattered about on the floor of each tier. He reached out to grab a puzzle after he saw that Kabe was already holding one. Kabe was pulling and tugging at the puzzle, and as Everett examined his puzzle, he realized that it was a series of rings stuck together in a cluster.

Glancing discreetly at Kabe's puzzle, he realized that their puzzles were different. He turned to scan the room, searching for Greta. Just as the lights dimmed, he saw her sitting a few rows below him. There was no time to get her attention or to move, so he sat back on his cushion with a disappointed frown on his face.

The dimming of the lights ended the soft conversations in the room, and an expectant hush filled the room. A single light turned on over the platform, and to Everett's surprise, a young man walked out. He smiled and waved at the full room as he sat down on a stool.

"Good evening. My name is Ethan, and I am a MASTERY student that studies sustainable engineering. You have been invited to this seminar because your instructors have noticed a quality in you that they would like to continue to develop. They have noticed that you *persevere*. That means that when you decide to do something, you have a will to master the task, no matter what the challenges or frustrations, no matter how long it takes. Please take a moment to consider when your instructors might have noticed this trait in you."

The audience became still as they pondered the young man's words. Everett's face puckered as he tried to think of why he might have received this invitation. It made sense to him immediately when he thought of Kabe and Greta. They were both very focused and driven in everything that they did.

Everett did not see that quality in himself. Although he could concentrate on projects when he was really interested, he tended to lose focus and move from one activity to the next when left to his own devices. He also continued to struggle with his urge to avoid tasks that were difficult or that he did not know how to start, so he didn't understand what an instructor might have seen in him.

"Ms. Everlay probably recommended you because of your plant experiment," Kabe whispered to Everett.

Hmm, Everett thought. *I guess I did stick to that project, even when it was challenging, but I don't know if that is why I am here.*

"I hope that you have all reflected and have figured out why you were invited to this SEMINAR. I would like to tell you a little about one of my experiences with this trait. I started at The School for Gifted Potentials when I was thirteen. That is a bit older than when most children start here, but I did not start late because I lacked POTENTIAL, it was because I was traveling around the world with my parents. Everywhere that we went, I paid attention to how people grew food, how they got and used energy, and how they maximized resources. It is an obsession that I still have today," Ethan said with a shrug.

Everett and Kabe exchanged a glance, both thinking that it was an interesting topic.

"So at some point, I started thinking about rain. How to harvest it, how to store it, how to utilize it. I started drawing pictures of all the different methods for rain collection that I saw, in all of the places that we traveled to."

He gestured behind him and images of his sketches appeared for the audience to see. Most of the pictures contained labels and notes about the apparatus, so he let most of the images speak for themselves. Every once in a while, Everett could tell that a particular image would excite Ethan, because he would describe it to the audience and explain how it worked. Finally, regretfully, he waved the images away.

"Sorry, I could talk about this all day. During my ORIENTATION, I was asked to set a long-term goal. I set a goal to design a way to collect and store rainwater in the structure of a building. I feel strongly that if each building can gather and store rainwater, and if the rainwater can be filtered and pumped into the building, we will have a sustainable way to harvest drinking water, which will decrease our impact on the environment."

He paused as the audience began to murmur, and a smile lit up his face when he realized that they liked his idea. Greta twisted around, searching for Everett in the dark auditorium. When their eyes connected, they shared a smile, both interested in Ethan's idea.

"During my ORIENTATION, I thought that I would accomplish this goal in one year. I thought that with my knowledge about the topic of rain collection, I would easily devise a contraption or a material that could gather and store rainwater without damaging the structure of a building," Ethan continued. "Over the years, I have invented over *three hundred* different possible solutions. Each one took a lot of time and research to create. Sometimes I designed a device and then made it using several different materials, while other times I tested one material with several different designs. In particular, I have tried over two hundred ways to collect and hold water on the roof of a building, because I believe that the roof will be the most effective location to gather rainwater. It has been a long journey."

He paused again, and Everett leaned forward, sure that Ethan was about to wave his hand at the screen to show them what he had finally created. Everett had no doubt that the MASTERY student must have devised a solution, and he was curious to find out what the solution was.

"I have still not designed something that works," Ethan said after a long pause, and several students in the audience gasped.

"I haven't given up, though," he continued, holding up his hand, "and I am still working on new designs. You see, despite the challenges, despite the frustrations, I have a *will* and a determination to see this through. It is easier to stay focused on this invention because I have a passionate interest in it, but I can also say that learning to persevere on this project has helped me in other areas of study. I have learned to cope with frustration and to discipline myself to take critique and failure and use them to spark new ideas."

Everett suddenly grinned, realizing that he had persevered on his technical writing assignment. He had taken each critique from his instructor and had rewritten and improved his writing several times. It felt good to understand why he had been selected for the seminar.

"You can discipline yourself to apply this trait, which comes so easily in tasks that interest you, to tasks that you have less interest or skill in. I hope that you noticed the wooden puzzles scattered around the room. These puzzles are yours to master. I want you to spend some time each day to try to solve one. Each puzzle has a shape or a variety of shapes that need to be straightened, and they all look deceptively simple. I hope that you will learn to embrace the challenge that they bring without frustration. They are my gift to you, as you continue your studies, to remind you that you have the strength and the drive to stick with any challenge that you set for yourself. I will let you know when I am successful in *my* quest," Ethan finished, giving the audience a confident grin and a wave.

The audience began to rustle as soon as he finished talking. Some students turned to talk to their neighbors about their puzzle, while others looked around for one, since they had not noticed the puzzles when they sat down.

Greta worked her way up the tiers toward Everett and smiled when she noticed Kabe sitting next to him. She folded her skirt under her knees and sat down next to Everett, showing him her puzzle. Kabe nodded a brief hello and then set to work on his puzzle, tugging and pulling at the pieces to straighten them out, only to find that he was causing the pieces to become even more tangled. Greta approached her puzzle more cautiously, pulling carefully at a few pieces and stopping to reflect on the progress that she made. Everett cradled the puzzle on his forearms so that he could resist the temptation to begin pulling at it. He studied the rings with his eyes, thinking that he could solve the puzzle with just one tug, *if* he tugged on the right ring.

He shared his idea with his friends, but Kabe merely grunted and did not take his eyes off his puzzle, which was becoming more tangled each time that he touched it. Greta tore her eyes away from her puzzle long enough to give him an encouraging nod, and then quickly went back to her careful manipulation of the puzzle rings. Everett sighed and continued his contemplation of the puzzle. He knew that this would drive him to distraction until he solved it, but he remembered that he was supposed to work on coping with his frustration as he did so.

Several students left the auditorium with their puzzles, but most of the students stayed to quietly work on their puzzles. After almost an hour had passed, one student at the front of the auditorium stood up and loudly announced that he was going to head to the dining hall for food, before his obsession with the puzzle made him waste away from hunger and thirst. The other students in the room chuckled, and many of them stretched as they stood up to leave.

Everett, Kabe, and Greta looked sheepishly at one another, their rumbling stomachs telling them to put their puzzles away and get some nutrition. They walked out of the auditorium together, following the other students in the general direction of the dining hall.

"So Kabe, how are you and Kimin getting along now?" Greta asked quietly. "I know that you both said that you aren't upset anymore, but it seems like you never really talk to each other."

Kabe shrugged and said, "I don't know. I don't have the EMOTIONAL OE, so I'm not holding on to any hurt feelings from our disagreement, although Kimin probably is. I just don't feel free to be myself with her. I feel like she has expectations about what a friendship should be like, and she doesn't allow us to be who we are or react to things the way that we want to. It also bothers me that she always thinks that she is right."

Greta and Everett were silent as they thought about his words. Kimin did seem to have expectations about how everything should happen, and she did not cope well with disappointment when her expectations were not met.

"Don't we *all* always think that we are right though?" Everett asked Kabe finally.

Kabe and Greta stopped walking, and the trio turned to look at each other.

"Yes... I mean we all have our own ideas and opinions," Kabe replied slowly, trying to find a way to explain what he meant. "But let's say that you and I both read a book, and I liked it, and you didn't. We would probably discuss the book, and try to convince each other to have the same opinion, but in the end, we would be okay with having a difference of opinion. I think that in the same situation, Kimin would just get really angry that I didn't see the book the same way that she does and would just say that I am wrong."

Everett nodded. It was a subtle difference, but it was the root of most of the problems that his small group had experienced.

"All right, so if Kimin struggles with always needing to be right, how do we help her with that?" he finally asked, knowing instinctively that a good friend would help Kimin with her problem rather than turn his back on her for it.

Kabe reddened slightly with embarrassment as he realized that Everett was right, and the trio slowly continued to the dining hall deep in thought.

Unexpected Choices

Everett and Greta hurried to their life science class the next morning. Ms. Everlay had announced that she was taking a leave of absence and that a new instructor would be assigned to the class. As they entered the classroom, several students were clustered around a tall woman with dark hair.

"I can't see her," Greta complained with a shrug.

Everett did not need to see her face to know who the woman was. His heart leapt into his throat as he realized that the new instructor was his mother.

"All right students, I am very glad to have met you, but I'd like for you to begin to find your stations," Camilla said laughingly. He could see that she was searching the room for him.

When their eyes met, electricity filled the space between them.

His eyes hardened.

Emotions bounced through him. His feelings changed from relief, to confusion, to anger. She had left him at the SFGP with no explanation. She had lied to him about who she was, and about who he was. He would forgive her eventually, he knew, but at this moment he wanted to show her how much she had hurt him.

She moved over to his side and smiled kindly at Greta.

"Good afternoon," Camilla said softly, her eyes flicking between Greta and Everett. "I am your new instructor, Dr. Grey."

Greta felt the strange tension between her friend and the new instructor and smiled awkwardly as she moved out of their way.

At last, Camilla turned to face Everett.

"Good afternoon. I have heard so much about you and your experiment with the Mars vegetation," she said, her eyes rapidly searching his for signs of his feelings. "Your experiment was incredible, and you should be proud of what you accomplished. I am excited that I will be working with you."

She reached out habitually to touch the hair on his forehead, and her hand snapped back as if she had been bitten when she realized that it was gone.

"You changed your hair," she whispered, sounding almost breathless.

"I have changed a lot of things," he replied bitterly and moved past her to find his seat.

He saw that she had to take a moment to compose herself, and a surge of regret filled his chest at the sight, but he quickly squashed the feeling. He told himself that what she was feeling was nothing like the emotions that he had been grappling with since his testing day at The School for Gifted Potentials, when the Chancellor had told him that his mother had signed away her rights to him.

Camilla sniffed and forced a bright smile onto her face as she turned to address the class.

"I have reviewed your experiments," she began brightly, "and you will *each* find a message from me tonight with an evening assignment. I have given each of you an area to improve on and I will be looking for your corrections throughout the week. For your lesson today, I have an experimental design for you to review. It is an example of an experiment that I designed and worked on as a MASTERY student. I would like for you to work together to find my flaws and show me what I could have fixed."

She smiled as the students began to chat with excitement. They had never gotten to inspect their last instructor's lab designs and the challenge excited them. Everett moved to Greta's side, and they worked together for the next hour to find ways to improve Dr. Grey's experimental design. After weeks of receiving critiques and feedback from his instructors, it was cathartic to find flaws in someone else's work, especially his mother's. He noticed that his mother repeatedly snuck looks in his direction as she walked around the classroom, but he did not give her the satisfaction of acknowledging her.

At the end of the class, as he moved out of the classroom with the rest of the students, Everett could not help but look back at her. She was standing at the back of the room, craning her neck over the other students' heads to find him. Some of his bitterness faded when he saw tears sparkling in her eyes.

A part of him panicked as he realized that this could be the last time that he saw her, that she could disappear from his life again. What if he lost her again, after he had been missing her all this time?

Indecision racked him, but Greta called out to him to hurry, and he turned back to the hallway, vowing to seek out his mother to talk to her about his abandonment as soon as he could.

Greta invited Everett to the rec center, which surprised him because she usually ran back to her room right after their class to work on assignments. His eyes narrowed as he wondered if she had noticed the tension between him and their new instructor, and then he sighed. If she suspected the truth anyway, it was probably time for him to admit it to her.

He thought that they would head to the Nature Center, but she grabbed his wrist and pulled him to the right as they entered the rec center. He noticed a series of doors and grinned when she pulled one open. This was a section of the rec center that he had not explored yet, and he was excited to see what was on the other side of the door.

There was a long padded bench and a soft armchair in the small room, and Greta gestured at them to indicate that he should pick one. Hesitantly, he selected the chair and sat down.

Greta tapped a few things on a control panel, and the walls were suddenly a continuous image of a sunset. She tapped again, and the peaceful sound of running water filled the room.

Satisfied, she sat cross-legged on the bench and leaned forward, waiting for him to look at her before she started to speak.

Finally, he glanced up at her, and she held his gaze.

"Sometimes I come in here because I just need some time alone. I sit in here and daydream, or I think about my parents, or about my friends," she said, emphasizing the last word.

"You think about your parents?" he asked quickly, trying to turn the conversation around to her, suddenly nervous that she would ask him about his parents despite his resolve to tell her the truth.

"Of course I do. You know, my parents do not agree with the residency requirement at this school. I would have had to stay here most of the time, since they live so far away, but I could have gone home for the holidays, or just whenever I needed to see them, if the residency policy had not changed," she said, her voice wobbling. "I worry that they are missing me, or that they are regretting that they sent me here. I try to work extra hard in my classes, because I want this experience to be *worth* losing my family, you know?"

She searched his face, looking for a sign that he understood. He surprised them both when a sob escaped him. Hot tears poured from his eyes as he connected with her words. It was as if she had reached into his jumble of emotions and had eloquently expressed them for him, only they were her emotions as well. Tears rolled down her face as well when she realized that he understood her.

He sniffed, and she handed him a tissue.

"Thank you," he said softly, looking down. "Yes, I know exactly what you mean. I was never supposed to be a student here. My mother tried to keep me away for so long, and then I got caught by an Observer and was forced to test here. I sabotaged the test, answered a bunch of things wrong that I knew were right, and I even told the Chancellor that I didn't want to go here. After all that, I found out that my mother had left me here and that she had signed papers that meant that I had to stay, even if I didn't want to. So I have been struggling with my feelings about her."

Greta sucked in a lungful of air, surprised by Everett's story. She knew that he was unsure about the school and that he had been dealing with emotions that he did not want to talk about, but she had never known the magnitude of what he was grappling with.

"You are so brave," she breathed, not even realizing that she spoke aloud.

His eyebrows shot up, and he released a small laugh filled with doubt. She flushed when she realized that she had spoken out loud, but his reaction spurred her to continue.

"No, really Everett, I never knew that you were here against your will. I find it amazing that you have put so much effort into making friends and that you have worked so hard in your classes, despite what your mother did. If that had happened to me, I don't know what I would have done," she shared, her voice thick with admiration.

If only I could tell you that you just met her, that she actually lied to me about her identity my whole life, that the Chancellor is my uncle, and that I suspect that Landon Perry is my father.

Instead of telling her the rest of his story, he smiled at her and leaned back in the chair, making it look as though he wanted to look at the sunset. Feeling satisfied that her friend had finally unloaded the emotional burden that he carried; she straightened her skirt and lay down to look at the sunset with him, unaware that there was so much more to his story that he had not shared.

Everett got back to his room that night, not sure what he would find. Part of him wondered if his mother would be in his room, perhaps looking at his posters, or sitting at his table. When the door opened and he saw an empty room, he felt both relief and disappointment. He had already eaten dinner with his friends in the dining hall, avoiding the inevitable message that waited for him from his new instructor, Dr. Grey.

Would she act casual on the message, as if he was any other student? Would she say something about why she had left him?

Shaking with anticipation, he saw the blinking message light and pressed *accept*. His mother's face filled the screen, and he pressed his hand to her cheek.

"Everett, my son," she began, her voice breaking. "I know that you must have a lot of questions about why you saw me in your classroom today. I am not sure what they told you about why you are here or what you might have discovered about me, so I am going to start by telling you the story of my past, the story that you never heard."

She broke off for a moment and looked away, and he wondered if she was ashamed that she had lied to him all this time.

"I was born to two loving parents, and I had an older half-brother that attended this school. He and I were never very close. He only came home on weekends, and he had a strained relationship with our father, but I admired him and hoped to become his friend someday. He loved the SFGP and always told me how amazing it would be for me to attend the school, but my parents had decided to keep me at home until I showed a need for acceleration. Just before my sixth birthday, my mother died. Father and I both had the EMOTIONAL OVEREXCITABILITY, and losing her was difficult for both of us. I dealt with her death by clinging to my father, but he dealt with it by pushing me away. My brother had been pressuring him for some time to enroll him at the SFGP as a full-time student, and one night my father came to me and told me that the following day, my brother and I would be enrolled at the SFGP as permanent residential students. I would never get to return home. My heart was broken."

She frowned, and Everett felt a surge of anger, because she had broken his heart by placing him there as well.

"My first few months at the school were difficult, although I did make a friend named Landon that helped me through the transition, as I am sure that you found a friend to help you adjust to life at this school. I saw very little of my brother. He checked in on me every once in a while, but he was not the supportive role model that I had expected. We drifted our separate ways as we got older. He threw himself into his field of study, and I threw myself into mine."

She paused for a moment to blow her nose, obviously having a difficult time with what she was recounting.

"As I grew up here, I felt lost. I felt like I had not gotten the nurturing that I needed. Although I thrived in my classes and loved the challenge, I also craved the comfort and support of a parent. I grew up wishing that my father had given me the option to attend the school *and* live at home. My friends filled some of the void, though, and Landon and I soon became an inseparable couple. I am sure that they took you to see the Life and Natural Sciences Wing. Landon and I, and our friends, were responsible for the creation of it. Landon and I had planned to work in Asia together after our MASTERY studies were over, and we secretly got married as soon as we completed our studies. We wanted to be able to leave for Asia the minute that we got our G tattoos."

Everett swallowed. Even though he had figured out that Landon Perry was his father, it still felt strange to hear his mother say it.

"Unfortunately, my brother had just become the Chancellor of the school and had changed the residency requirements. He *required* every student to live at the school full-time. I knew that he had changed the rule to suit himself, because he'd had a difficult time going home to our father, and I protested to everyone that would listen that his rule should be changed. I suggested to Landon that we both give up our G tattoos to show that we were against his decision, but Landon didn't agree that it would do any good."

She took a deep shuddering breath and looked straight into the camera.

"Landon Perry is your father Everett. I want you to know that I never told him about you. I was angry with him for not protesting with me, and I left him. Once I left, I did not know how to repair our relationship. I raised you with all the love that I have in my soul. You are my everything. I know that you must be wondering why I raised you to stay away from this school and then left you here. You hated your EDUCATIONAL EXPERIENCES, and I felt like you were making the decision to stay with me because you loved me, but also because you had never known anything else. If I had given you the choice, you would never have given the SFGP a chance. I had to let you experience the rigor and the challenge of this school, so that you could find out if learning this way suits you, and to give you the chance to make friends that are like you."

He nodded, knowing that she was right. If he had not felt trapped, he never would have given the school a chance.

"I don't know how you feel about this school," she continued with a sly grin, "but unlike the other students that are here, I have made it possible for *you* to have a choice. I did not sign any papers to relinquish my rights to you Everett."

He rocked back, blown away by her statement. The Chancellor had told him that his mother had signed away her rights and had left him. It had never occurred to him that his mother had left him as a way of circumventing the school's residency requirement.

"So now you have the choice Everett. I have secured a temporary position here, so if you want to stay, we can be near each other. It will never be the same as living together, but at least you can go to school here and have me in your life. If you want to come home to me, I can take you back at any time. I wanted to do this for you Everett, to give you the choice that I never had. I want you to always know that I love you. There has not been a decision that I have made that has not been in your best interest. I know that you might resent me for the way that I did it, but you could never have had this choice if I had not tricked you. I love you Everett. You are so special."

Her voice cracked and her image disappeared.

Hearing her explanation, Everett knew that she had done her best to give him an impossible choice. She was right that if she had not left him there, he would never have given The School for Gifted Potentials a chance. He would never have learned about himself as a gifted learner in this way, would never have known the thrill of learning in this way, and would never have made such unique and talented friends.

She had thwarted her brother's residency only decree by finding a way to let him attend the school with the option of leaving. No other student at The School for Gifted Potentials had that power.

Now that he had it, he had to decide what he would do with it.

Author's Note

Although I was labeled a gifted learner in elementary and took "different" classes as I got older, no one ever explained what the word gifted meant to me, and over the years it slowly lost any meaning. Through a series of unintended and fortuitous events, I was recruited into a Master's program for gifted education.

In my first class, I read a chapter that discussed Dabrowski's Overexcitabilities, which utterly transformed my self-concept. I realized that no gifted child should have to wait until adulthood to understand what gifted means and that every gifted child should learn how to embrace the power of the traits that they are born with. I hope that The School for Gifted Potentials series provides an understanding of self to the next generation of gifted, as well as to previous generations that want to understand more about their gifted characteristics.

The following resources were used in researching this book:
Austega.com. Ed. David Farmer. 1995. Web. Mar. 2012.
<http://www.austega.com/>. Used with permission.

SENG. Ed. Lisa Rivero. Supporting Emotional Needs of the Gifted, 2011. Web. 12 Jan. 2012. <http://www.sengifted.org/>. Used with permission.

Discussion Questions

1. Did Everett use all of the managing strategies that he learned in his ORIENTATION?
2. Which OVEREXCITABILITY does Everett struggle with the most?
3. Which OVEREXCITABILITY does Everett struggle with the least?
4. Everett has the EMOTIONAL OVEREXCITABILITY, but Kabe does not. How does this difference affect the way that they experience things?
5. How do the classes and opportunities at the SFGP help each student reach their POTENTIAL?
6. Camilla did not take her G tattoo to protest her brother's residency requirement, but Landon thought that the protest would not change anything. Who do you think was right? Why do you think that?
7. Kimin was upset with Kabe and Everett for not listening to her and told them that she did not want to be friends any longer. How do you think she could have handled the situation differently?
8. The Chancellor believes that the children that live at the school are happier because they are constantly surrounded by people that understand their needs, and uses his daughter's success at the school as proof that his residency requirement works. What evidence have you found that he may be wrong?
9. Greta and Everett both struggle with the need to be perfect, but they each have their own coping strategy. How do you cope with the need to be perfect?
10. Camilla has given Everett an unexpected choice. What do you think he should choose to do? Why do you think that?

61948368R00096

Made in the USA
Lexington, KY
29 March 2017